letters
to a
loved one

letters
to a
loved one

Hannah Duffy

gatekeeper press™
Tampa, Florida

Letters to a Loved One

Published by Gatekeeper Press
2167 Stringtown Rd, Suite 109
Columbus, OH 43123-2989
www.GatekeeperPress.com

Library of Congress Control Number: 2022947393

ISBN (paperback): 9781662929694

First, a special thanks to:

My parents, Laurie and Chris, who told me that a dream is the reason to keep going. A dream is a reason to get up everyday, a dream is a progression through life, and your help with this story was my dream.

My grandparents, the first readers of this, and the ones that read with me. Your stories will always be my favorite stories to hear. Thanks for being in my book club.

Sarah Shriber, who made the process as easy as breathing. This is pretty life changing for me. Thank you for going above and beyond what I even thought.

All of my friends, who argued with me over every detail of this story, and sat with me as I wrote it. You were sitting beside me as I wrote the last line. That meant a lot.

To my twin sister, Molly. I write all my letters to you.

dear loved one,

I have told this story, this urban legend, to friends of a friend. I have
written it down a thousand times, in thoughts and conversations, in paint
and pencil. I have brought a flashlight to my mouth and spoken in the
dark, and the words were never right. It is but a simple story. And so now,
I will start it by saying that September had never been so tiring as it was
in 1945.

September was a tiring month in 1945, it was true, but in years
past, it was a month of renewal. In years past, there was no war to attend
to and clean up after. In years past, people mailed their letters full of
beautiful things without a worry that they would never receive one in
return. They wrote of their homes brimming with peace and the salty
air of a summer ending, of newborn children and marriages. But 1945
was a year for broken traditions. The mail was sent discreetly, then with
trepidation, and finally with guilty relief. September brought that guilty
relief. It brought tales of a war buried into the ground. It brought coffins
on trains to the graveyards, where people stood about and listened,
thinking, "Thank God it wasn't me. Thank God it wasn't me."

There were two sides to September that year. There was the
winning side and there was the losing. On the second of the month,
people were beginning to forget which side they had claimed as their
own. The winners were shouting with victory, then they were nursing
their brothers, who were limping from the bullets in their legs. The losers
contented themselves with distraction, and while sweeping their bombed-
out cities, they thought, "At least we weren't the only ones." You would see
it happening around you; the houses were lived in, but only half of them
were lit. There was the hum of the radio from your neighbor's house, but
down the street, it fell quiet. Some were waiting for the announcement
because surely, surely after years of fighting, it was over now. And some
were waiting for a death sentence.

But there was a town, a lonely, lovely town, where it was
different. It was all quiet. The people didn't celebrate, for they had never

particularly fought. And the population was generally uplifted, although one man could not be mistaken for such. On this night, he was sitting outside his home, his car running, with the September air bleak and cold, and he celebrated the loss of a friend. What a good friend he had had. There is no loss comparable to that of losing a friend.

"To you," he said to the silence, raising his hand to the imagined painting of his friend. "And you, and you, you, you, you." Soon the picture of his friend was heavy with others, people he had never seen before, and there were too many to toast. He let his hand fall.

I have told this story, this urban legend, to friends of a friend. I will start by saying that September had never been so tired as it was in 1945.

March, 1945.

1

Born with great solitude and despair, Telly Leone was excited to have finally made a lifelong friend. He wasn't excited to hear that his friend was leaving.

Their friendship began in Boston at the early age of nine, during a street fight between three young boys. Rico Romano was immediately deemed the loser as he was outnumbered two to one by these ferocious little rascals that he knew by name; they were, after all, his classmates and neighbors. None of the boys ever had the opportunity to be friends, as Rico's father was slightly discriminatory toward those of non-Italian descent, and one of the bullies had a British mother (it was assumed; she had the accent) whom the neighborhood despised for her ungodly cooking. In the first week of 1927, a year before the street fight, the neighborhood woke to find the mother's Great Britain flag splashed with cooked pasta shells and some kind of sauce that one could smell for days after.

Telly was simply returning home from school that day, and he passed an alley where he heard angry grunts and the whizzing of fists in the air. Taking a shy look in, he saw three boys he recognized, two swinging at the one. Telly's first instinct told him to keep walking. His parents were inside his head telling him that it would be stupid. And because of this, he dropped his books and soared into the mess wailing and waving his fists, and soon the storm had subsided, with all four boys on the ground and the two bullies supremely defeated on their way home. Telly jumped to his feet with buoyancy and pride, helped the other boy up, and told him he'd better not get into fights anymore.

"I didn't start the fight," said the boy. "They called on me."

"Oh. I don't see what you can do to stop that but try, because I don't want to have to do that for you every time now."

"I didn't *ask* you to help me. I think I did a nice job."

"Do you have a nickel? I have to charge you for the rescue."

"I'm not allowed to give money to strangers."

From then on, it was Rico and Telly, Telly and Rico. They were best friends through all of life's travels, even ending up residing in the same town in their twenties, our mystery town of the decade. They were both the strange age of twenty-six, Rico married, living in a nice home with three children. His oldest, Frank, was made Telly's godson. He had himself two daughters as well, one four years and the other nine months. Their average-sized home was not five blocks from Telly.

Now, Telly began most days the same way. Each morning he woke at 7:30 to his radio blaring, for he preferred to keep it on while sleeping. He dressed nicely and took his briefcase with him two towns over, where he taught an hour and a half lecture on 19th century art to college students. He had begun the course teaching regularly, but by October he noticed his class was dwindling surely. By March, Telly had twelve everyday students. At ten a.m. when his class had been dismissed, he retired home, changed out of his work clothes, gathered his talent, and headed toward the richest neighborhood in town, where he tutored several of the high schoolers living there. Their parents paid well, and although Telly's midday company was of random teenagers who did not earn much from his help, he never minded. His degrees of sorts were related to education and arts, but now was hardly the correct moment to join a school's staff permanently.

By 3:30, he busied himself at home with whatever was there for him. Most days he worked on his art. Telly had a large canvas in his small living room, stretching 14x20, propped up on an easel. Telly was an artist. As I am not, I cannot describe the way he painted and breathed in with better than moderate talent. He simply awoke one day, discovered his abilities, and made the decision to never put down a paintbrush again. He grew taller and smaller with every color and when he closed his eyes, he did not see the standard blurriness of black, but splotchy bright colors that have never been invented. He only bled the brightest reds or blacks and could picture their exact names on a bottle. When he drank, if he drank, it was never to forget but to recall.

He spent some of his time like this. Other days, Telly would run simple errands, visit neighbors or friends, have the occasional drugstore date or two. On this particular March day, the sun shone brilliantly, a golden dome above the people, and the wind cut skin. There was still snow on the ground. It was past 3:30, and Telly was just outside his best friend's door.

Warm and maternal, Carrie was the older sister Telly never had. She opened the door of her home immediately at his arrival and gestured him in. Rico and Carrie's house was sturdy and fit for children, with leaky walls that released the smell of her cooking out onto the streets. Telly smelled the cookies in the oven at the first moment.

"What're you cooking?" he asked because it was polite.

"Cookies, dear. C'mon in, Rico is in the study with the kids." She grinned ear to ear. She was twenty-five years old, and already had a severe motherly love afflicted on her by three little things.

Down the hallway (scattered with Lincoln Logs and sewn dolls) was Rico's office, the last door on the right. Carrie knocked gently, her face closest to Telly as it had ever been, and he could see the freckled youth his best friend had fallen in love with before everything shot to hell.

"Shh," hissed Rico from inside the office. He had been working at home for Carrie's sake lately. "I've got Ines in here asleep and Donna and Frank are playing some game. They slap each other's hands and then they flick at each other's faces; it's really competitive."

"Hi, Rico," Telly said.

"Oh, it's Telly. I remember you were coming over. Come inside now, very, very quiet, the door squeaks—"

Sitting in a wooden rocking chair behind his desk was Rico in a robe over his office suit, holding his nine-month-old daughter Ines in his lap, who stirred peacefully.

"Hi," he whispered.

Carrie joined Frank, their oldest, beside the green floral curtains, where he was playing pattycake on the floor with his sister, Donna, whose head began to loll back.

"I'll get the kiddies," said Carrie. She wound Ines into her arms without a cry from the baby's mouth and helped Donna from the room. Rico thanked her and shut the door.

"Lemme see Frank," Telly cried excitedly. He tried very hard not to show it, but his nephew was his favorite of Carrie and Rico's kids. He was a bright boy who had only just turned five, who wore striped shirts and strappy overalls, and who had bony fingers that liked to touch things he ought not to. Frank especially enjoyed blocks, watching his father on the telephone, his mother's hair, and his "uncle," who visited often.

"Hey, Tell." Frank punched the knees of Telly, who stopped to be face to face.

"Have you gotten into much trouble yet?" he asked.

"Nope, ask Dad."

Rico shrugged. "He's into building things, you know."

"Well, maybe he'll be a constructor," said Telly.

"Constructor?"

"It's a job where you build things, Frank. You'd like that," said Rico.

"Tell, are you... what you said?"

"Nope," said Telly. "I'm an artist, remember. Or a painter. Whatever you'd like to call me."

"D'you know who painted Lady Liberty?"

"I know the constructor who built it. Frédéric Auguste Bartholdi, say that name ten times fast," said Telly.

"You're buddies with him?"

"He's like a thousand years old, Frankie," Rico informed. "Telly doesn't know him, he knows *of* him."

"No, no, don't listen there, Frank. Me and this man, Mr. Bartholdi, are good friends."

Frank tugged at his father's hand. "That's neat."

"I think so too."

"Go out with Mama, Frankie," Rico told him. "Me and Tel will be out in a minute."

Telly opened the door for Frank and watched his nephew run down the hallway to the kitchen, where, undoubtedly, the cookies had finished baking.

"I love New England. I love Massachusetts," said Rico, turning to his friend.

"I do too."

"No, I'm really glad we live here. We've got a son who's already seen the Statue of Liberty. I think that's a nice accomplishment. He wouldn't have seen it living in the south."

"I think I thought Lady Liberty was less important as a child. The only statues we saw were better in my eyes."

"I loved old Georgie when we were kids. I liked his horse."

"Horses freaked me out."

"Carrie wants to move," said Rico suddenly. He leaned forward and cupped his chin in his hands. "She wants to move. I can't think of a reason why not to move except because of you or the draft."

Telly was silent for a moment. His brain hurt slightly, twinged, and winced. Then he spoke up. Something in his friend's narrative confused him.

"The draft?"

"Yes, the draft, *of course*, the draft." Rico wrung his hands together agitatedly, his fingernails scratching to make him wince. "I nearly forgot about the thing, Telly, I wish I had. *Carrie* must have."

"The draft won't hurt him," promised Telly. "Frank's only a little one. This whole thing will be over soon. And you can't be drafted either, cause of Jesse and—"

"Marvin. Yeah. Makes me sort of lucky, huh?"

Jesse and Marvin were Rico's older twin brothers. Rico never met the pair, as they were away in the first war the day he was born, and died too, but because of the sad thing, Rico was the sole surviving son and would not be eligible for the draft. His smart job helped as well. It was very helpful to the people and almost, but not quite, very needed.

I had met the brothers once. They were among the few who smiled at my presence.

"They'll get me," he said. "They'll get me and in a couple of years, they'll get my boy."

"It's against the law."

"Is it, Telly? Are you positive they can't get me? This thing hasn't ended yet, Telly. Who's to say there won't be another fourteen years of it?"

"Well, the government, the economy, the shrinking armies—"

"Well, what if they lower the age-eligible? I will not have my fifteen-year-old boy holding a rifle. I won't have it."

"It won't happen, Rico," Telly maintained. "It will not."

Rico slumped in his chair, his distressed state fizzing down to exhaustion. He could hear his wife and children just down the hall from him, giggling and shouting and attempting to stay quiet, all for him. Under his dark, flickering eyes, his circles were a magnifying old mauve purple. Telly wondered many things about his friend's appearance, and how many nights he had stayed up arguing with his conscientious, naturally lighthearted conscience.

"I wonder, do you have Jesse or Marvin's eyes?"

"Huh?"

"I said, I wonder if you have Jesse or Marvin's eyes?" repeated Telly.

"I don't know," mumbled Rico. "Suppose I've got my dad's."

"D'you know what Jesse and Marvin's eyes looked like?"

"I've got the broad idea from pictures, but to see someone's eyes you need to see them in person."

"That's right."

The friends jumped at the sudden clatter of pans. Carrie called to them, "I'm making supper, Rico. Watch the kids for me?"

Telly and Rico left his office door ajar and went to greet his wife. Telly swept his coat buttoned and politely declined to stay; he was not very hungry and he gripped his nephew's hand. It was very soft and baby-like, warm like his mother, and released bits of youthful joy into Telly. He smiled one more time and left the house. Across the globe at that exact moment, I oversaw battles that lasted for weeks. Telly never learned the details.

2.

It was an odd thought to have, but Mckenzie knew his fourteen-year-old self would despise him at eighteen. And he would be eighteen in only a few days.

Mckenzie Anthony Rye, born in an East Coast hospital at six a.m., March 11th.

His eighteenth birthday was in less than ten days.

Who, of even the most despicable personalities, could handle having the hatred of a fourteen-year-old boy on their conscious? Not Mckenzie, and his personality was barely up to par. True, he had never committed crimes of heinous abilities, nor stole or attacked undeserving civilians. He just fought those who he thought deserved it.

Born in a city residing just outside of New England, Mckenzie attended school there all up until his junior year. After refusing to complete assignments, and encouraging and getting into fights with those he deemed worthy of a throw, he was expelled by a much remorseful headmaster.

"You've made an excellent student, Mr. Rye," said his headmaster the day of his expulsion.

"Except for the fighting," Mckenzie said.

"Except for the fighting," he agreed.

This particular incident, like many previous, Mckenzie had gotten into a cynical argument with a boy he openly detested. At eighteen, Mckenzie could not remember the boy's name. But they fought with tongue and fists until teachers were brought to the scene. Both were brought to the office; both were expelled. Mckenzie was an exemplary student, despite his temper. His classmates grew tired of him turning his work in before a quarter of the hour was over; he grumbled answers under his breath and scorned that the work was too easy. Eventually, he left school up to fate.

Sure, he was disappointed. Mostly in the school's academic agenda, but his parents argued that his expulsion was the best thing for him and that he would do far better at a school with less control and tougher assignments. They were, as usual, correct. The family moved to town, and he attended school fluently for the rest of his high school experience. He listened to his lessons and never fought, not once. He took tutors up on their offers and learned of his talents. Again, as I said, Mckenzie's younger self would have hated his secondary school persona.

Mckenzie had few friends over the years; they could never stick. He was never too *anything* and had none of the defining qualities that you could call a good friend out on. He was exceptionally habitual, never having an outburst of personality. He was a quiet kid. And he hated that part. But eventually, Mckenzie assumed that this new school and town had brought out his true character, and decided being a quiet kid was his new destiny.

He was not so solemn around Telly.

—

At 3:32, for he was two minutes late, Mckenzie took notice, his tutor had arrived in the entrance hall of his family's Colonial. Mckenzie's parents, who worked until 5:00, left their son to return home from school by 3:00. There he patiently awaited further teaching, and his tutor let himself into the house.

Mckenzie quickly sat on the floor of his finished basement. Around him was the collection of art supplies he had accumulated over the years.

"Hey, you're late," he said to his tutor.

"Yes, I am," said Telly, and he genuinely seemed surprised. "Two minutes is fashionably late."

"It's not."

"That's not what Hollywood tells me," he said, sitting down beside his student. "You know they say that I've got that really famous

look, but I can't get their speech exactly right. What the hell is that?"
Mckenzie had by his side a handful of small colorful balloons.

"You fill them with paint, and tape them to the canvas and throw darts at them."

"Do you have darts?"

"We could use knives."

"I don't like the idea of you with a weapon. You might murder me."

"You're bringing it about yourself."

"I don't think your parents would be enthusiastic about me if I encouraged your painting delusions to end up on the floor."

"They aren't enthusiastic about you anyways, Telly. They think you're a little wild. And childish, maybe."

"Really?" He again looked genuinely surprised, yet unbothered. "Well. I thought they were sweet on me."

"No, no. Dad turns his head in the hardware store. He's got quite an eye for five-star screwdrivers, apparently."

"Phillip's heads are no good, I hear."

"Agree to disagree. So." Mckenzie nudged his 8x8 canvas in front of him. "What are we painting?"

"You're asking me?"

"Yeah. You're supposed to teach me."

"What do you want to know?"

"The secrets of life." Mckenzie grinned, scratching at the canvas.

"How's school going?" Telly asked. He suppressed the urge to lay on his back and stare up at the impressive ceilings. Mckenzie's parents had money whether they denied it or not, and Telly knew the look of wealth.

"Well. But that's not a secret."

"What am I supposed to teach you that you don't already know?"

"Whatever you were hired to, I guess."

"I hope you go to a good school, Mckenzie."

"I will," he said.

"Yeah, you will."

Mckenzie tapped out a pattern on his canvas. Some tune he had heard on the radio. "Are you really this bland around everyone else?"

"No. Well, I'm not being *bland* right now. I'm only wondering what else there is to teach you, because I think I've used up my knowledge on you. And you're too smart for your age. It's no good. Go indulge your mind with gory movies and drink liquor behind gas stations."

"I'll try and dumb down."

"So." Telly nudged Mckenzie's 8x8 canvas in front of him. "What are you painting?"

"I don't know yet. When I think of it, I'll let you know. Telly?"

"Yeah?"

"Telly, guess what?"

"I can't think of what to guess. Person, place, thing, or noun? That's not right."

"I turn eighteen soon."

"That!" said Telly, whirling around to Mckenzie. His dark pupil-less eyes were a wild mesh of lucidness and genius concoctions. "That! Paint that. Paint 'eighteen.'"

"The *number* eighteen?"

"No, no, no, no, no. The—er." His hand gestures became dramatically shaky and wide. "The feeling, the feeling you get when you turn eighteen."

"I don't know what the feeling is yet. I'm not eighteen."

"*Imagine.* Jesus. What do you think? No painting exists in your head without physically imagining its clothes."

"I don't know. Dread, I think."

"Peculiar!" Telly exclaimed. He leapt to his feet and opened his arms as if to embrace Mckenzie. His voice dropped its excitement. "Now why dread?"

"Because I'm seriously dreading turning eighteen. It's just dread. That's all."

"What the hell?" Telly frowned. "Why?"

"Are you questioning my emotions? You told me to imagine the feeling."

"You didn't have to. You already feel dread. What's up with that?"

"I think lots of kids feel dread on their eighteenth birthday."

"No, no. That's weird. Eighteen is a time of enlightenment."

"Is it really?"

"Yes, it is!" The wild, eccentric tone had returned to the tutor's voice, and his arms waved as he paced around the room. Mckenzie braced for a ranting.

"The greatest minds of our times, they touch eighteen, and then, on that day, their brains have only begun. The widest brushstroke on human history and intelligence is made by that above age. The mental capacity has reached a peak, you are no longer a child and yet you feel not like an adult, there's attention and yet none at all, all at once—you can see the expectations before you, and finally, you see the possibilities, and that, my friend, can strangle you. I know many about me that have been shown possibilities for them the size of a mouse and their lives are subpar and their world is subpar, for it includes none of the magic that eighteen is supposed to bring to you."

"Are you saying the mind develops at eighteen?"

"No, I'm saying you're an idiot."

"Is that your lesson for the day?"

"I don't know yet. I'll get back to you on that."

Mckenzie brushed his hair behind his ears. "Do you think you'd like to stay for dinner?"

"What's that?"

"Dinner? Would you like to stay for it? I believe we are having—I can't remember."

"Is that you asking me or your parents?"

"Both."

"Alright, I thank you, my hospitable student." Telly extended his hand out to shake, then quickly brought it back. "I accept *your* offer but I may have to decline your parents—I have heard that they apparently are *not* enthusiastic about me."

3.

Carrie Romano sat in her husband's office chair, and it was ten o'clock at night. Rico and her children had long retired to bed. He woke early in the mornings, drank too much coffee, and his high had filtered away by five. Their children were quiet. They cried little, something Rico was very amazed at. They slept sound in their beds, and now Carrie was alone, looking out the office window at their perfect suburbia. She thought it was too good to be true.

Early that day, she had seen some boys at the town hall. A group of them. All most likely eighteen. She knew they had to be at least legal and she pinpointed that age specifically, noting the way the boys huddled close but talked loud, whispered a little as well, and took turns swiveling around at the men who left the town hall doors. Carrie knew what they wanted. She wondered if they would get it.

In the afternoon, Carrie met a realtor in a house in a nice neighborhood, towns away. The realtor was kind. She opened the door for Carrie and wore nice work clothes that she said she had sewn herself. What a busy woman. She opened every door of the house for Carrie. Four bedrooms, three bathrooms. A finished basement, and a nice one at that. It was a house that should have been far beyond their means, but Rico had always been lucky in his line of work. He was liked very much by his bosses. They played poker some nights and Rico took up their drink offers, but only drank two. She knew he would continue in his profession if they moved. For years, he had been working at the same insurance company, following the practice around the state. Maybe he'd move to another office, make friends, and invite them over for dinner. They'd compliment Carrie's cooking, hold the little ones. One would drink too much; he'd sleep on their couch.

In the evening, Carrie came home and took off her shoes. She made dinner. Tidied a bit. Hugged her husband, who often took calls from home, and her children. Changed diapers. Prepared baths. She thought of moving. The packing of the boxes was so final, and the last click of the door would be the last time they'd hear that specific click. Her thoughts wandered. They went to the boys at the town hall, and she wondered if their ages had been guessed right, what their parents did and how they cooked and what they thought of their sons, and if they had any siblings. She wondered what the boys thought of themselves.

At ten o'clock, her family asleep, Carrie sat in her husband's office and thought of Telly. She thought of his job and his tutoring gigs, how his life was as connected to others as possible. She wondered how many boys he taught and if they made plans to confront their parents at dinner time, or simply let the idea blow over and forget about it. It was difficult, yet easy to forget. She remembered a kid Telly had mentioned as a favorite. He never blatantly said it, but Carrie could tell from how he didn't bother with any of the typical false praise. Carrie liked him from the stories. He was short of eighteen, and short of eighteen was a dangerous age, Carrie knew. Especially now. Especially at a time like this. Carrie wondered if this kid would join up, too. Would he confront his parents about it and would they cry or clap with pride or solemnly nod or angrily scream? Would he do it, she thought. And the moment it crossed her mind, she knew the deed was already done. It had happened years before the war started, years before this kid's birth. It was a slice of fate coming to life, Carrie thought. She prayed to God without being charismatic. A mantra spun in her head. She wondered again and again if he and the others would do it. I was in my world, a world where this had already happened and repeated a million times, and I alone knew the answer.

4.

At nine o'clock at night, a single-man fisherman had already retired to his cabins after a long day. The catch was small. The netting was knotted. Below deck, the letters of his family were scattered on the table. Evidently, he had fallen asleep reading such scriptures; he was face down to the wood with his forearms braced around his ears. The boat rocked. He felt disturbingly warm in his slumber.

The fisherman was middle-aged and married with a child. His beard was sculpted into a slight point at the end of his wide jaw, his teeth were of average size for such a face, his hair was pale brown. It was turning gray. His abnormally large ears were bent at a painful-looking angle but the fisherman did not appear to notice. He was far too asleep. Most weeks, the fisherman docked at ports along the East Coast. He made to dial his family and send his letters once on land. He picked up supplies he needed and took a newspaper along. At the beginning of the month, he had read of Pearl Harbor. He admired the state of Hawaii.

"Those Japs," he had thought. "Fucking bastards." He had sworn quite a bit and then fallen asleep fast. He had dreamt little and slept to the sound of the waves.

It had been hours since the sun had set. Still he was in deep sleep. The newspaper lay next to him. By eleven o'clock, the boat began to shake him awake. He blinked, his long jaw hung open, and he rubbed at his eyes until little lights appeared behind the eyelids. He coughed. He nudged his letters and held his newspaper. The ends had been bent. The fisherman skipped the first few pages, his tired string of a brain close to pulling apart, and began reading. There was one specific article he had taken to, on a page he forgot in the future, about a town with no draft. He read the entire article until he could not see the words anymore, for they had all blurred together and teetered on and off the page. He had never heard of such a town.

The fisherman deposited his paper on the table and returned to the top deck. The night was ghastly cold, the wind hyperpigmentation in his eyes of rainbow streaks. He could still see the stars. They were always clear off the coast. The smell of salt was too comforting to not smell of home. He leaned over his railing so he could see the dark sea, liquid wrath, hurtling itself against the side of his boat several feet down. The empty stairway to hell. He swore aloud, "Fucking bastards."

The next week, the fisherman returned home from his voyage. The winter would be too cold. He brought his suitcase to the front door of his house and hugged his wife and kid. He cried. And he never went out to sea again.

5.

As difficult as it sounded when the citizens moved to town, they understood the rules fairly quickly.

1. They knew they were lucky to live there.
2. They knew that anyone, after taking all that trouble to get to town, wouldn't want to move again. That would be insane.

Carrie and Rico, it seemed, were insane. At least by the standards of others. In 1941, they moved to town. And now, in '45, they wanted to *leave*. They couldn't *leave*. That would be insane.

There was only one defining law that other towns and states did not have. The rest of the rules were created in the minds of the citizens, never openly said out loud but understood in unison like the lyrics of an old song everyone heard, but didn't quite know the lyrics. Statistically speaking, it was the safest place on Earth, the richest and the luckiest. Men lived here and died here. They never died anywhere else. No one strayed. And there was no draft. That was the one defining law in town, the one unconcerned law in the most unconcerned place in all of America. No one took sides or made enemies; no contributions were made to the war. And there was no draft here.

But there were volunteers.

Telly himself grew up in Boston, an hour's drive from his future place of residence. Before 1940, the town was exceedingly average. There was no need for a protection zone, for there was nothing people had to be protected from. By 1940 there was tension between the so-called Huns, the Japs, the fresh-faced French, and the Tommys. Telly, who was still living in Boston at the time with Rico, witnessed several street fights between the young American boys who discovered the young Japanese or German children on their own. Camps were being built all along the coasts by the government, but their one duty to protect all citizens was given when the law was made. A town was chosen to be the sole loner, the neutrality in the harsh opinions opposing morally good and evil.

Each person had varying views, but in this chosen place, there would be no views to partake in. There would be no talk of war, no choosing sides or antagonizing others with different views. No harassing others on the other side. No draft. Guilting individuals into joining would be punishable by a fine or a night in the county jail. And there would be population control, a polite term for saying there could only be a certain number of people in residency. It was a strange resolution, an awkward situation but went rather smoothly despite what you may think.

Telly was twenty-two in '41, fresh out of an arts college his mother had recommended to him. He was essentially broke when he began working in Boston on parts for military aircraft. His only specialty was fighter planes, specifically the wing spars. His architectural fascinations were perhaps his only allowance for working on the machines. Somedays he would return to his flat and have a short conversation with his neighbor, who wore a titanium ring on her ring finger, and wondered how many attempts at bombing it would take to get the jewelry off, then hurry inside to look through the newspaper, searching for a photograph of a fighter he had contributed to, as if he would see the wing spar through the destructible material. In short, Telly liked his job enough to purely hate it and used it bitterly to keep himself alive. He wasn't one for building anything for that matter; he simply liked the way the glass panel windows let sunlight slip into patterns on the metal—a sight so soft it made the creaking and scraping of titanium less rough on the ears—and the way this job could almost guarantee his safety from the draft.

Of course, it wouldn't last long. It was Rico who found the town first in 1941, who learned of it from a buddy at the office, sipping moldy, watered-down coffee by the pot, as they huddled together like a club. There was a moment that Rico and Carrie thought together on the issue; he wanted to see his children grow up. The event that brought the couple and their friend away was Telly heading into the assembly line, wearing his strappy gloves early one morning, and being sent away with a cardboard box of his possessions with the apparent reason behind his layoff only being that he would be better useful somewhere in Europe, or in one of the planes with spars he had crafted himself.

"I'm in for it now," he told Rico over the telephone in a great state of depression. He paced back and forth; he tapped his foot erratically; he pulled the phone away from its base accidentally, letting it hang in the air suspended by the coil. His eyebrows were a straight line of stiffness.

"What the hell's wrong now? Well, I've been meaning to tell you that Carrie's due pretty soon—"

"I've been laid off. Fired. How long do I have, I wonder?" asked Telly. "Four days is my guess; and that's generous."

"You must be joking, Telly," said Rico.

"Wish I was."

Telly knew he had an unknown number of days before he was drafted, then sometime before he was shipped off on a bus full of brawny, eager men his age, and young seniors with caps on backward who had been gently encouraged onto the vehicle by their fathers. They would sing the choruses of God Bless America loudly and punch each other's shoulders and look at the trinkets and photographs the person beside them had brought, then the wheels would teeter over gravel and the bus would fall unnervingly quiet except for the occasional nervous whistle. That was how Telly pictured it would be.

The plan was created exceptionally quickly with several flaws they chose to look over. The trio figured it would be difficult to find standard living situations for all of them so quickly. There was the need for a job in Telly's case. And there was the dire problem of not needing to worry about the previous issues at all if somebody decided to accuse them of attempting to escape the law. If that happened, Telly would be drafted before he had time to unpack. But, incredibly, none of this appeared to be a problem.

Carrie, Rico, and Telly packed up their things and children and were able to move into a flat made for one in the haven town, using a collection of their savings put together. For only several days Carrie and Rico attended open house appointments, while Telly stayed home with the children and marveled at the neutrality in the East Coast setting. On street corners and overhead lamps there were no posters or donation centers. He bought himself a small canvas and a small set of new paints and received no judgment from the cashier on spending money that could have gone to a better cause. He was exceedingly happy for the few weeks Rico's children stayed with him all day. Telly propped his new canvas on a windowsill and painted the overcrowded living room, while one-year-old Frank pawed at the brushes. He loved those times, although they were short.

Eventually Carrie and Rico found a house right for them, only days before her baby was due. It was white and far bigger on the inside than it looked. It had strange lace-like patterns trimming the edges and the banister of the porch. There were two chimneys and little, badly cut bushes in the front. On New Year's, only four days after they had moved in, they were rushing out the door to the hospital, where the nurses did not comment on Rico's presence and where Carrie had a baby girl at 11:59 named Donna.

It was a happier place to be in with Rico and Carrie. Rico kept his very important job that Telly did not know much about, and Carrie almost fully forgot about the war and stopped reading the paper. They never watched the news, they kept their heads out of it all, never engaged in political talk or treated people of German or Japanese descent differently. Nobody in town did. It was like the war had never existed, which Telly was ready to enjoy believing. He worked at several jobs in town before deciding he wanted to go back to school, something he had dropped out of upon Pearl Harbor and the job building plane parts. Telly attended community college and soon met two extraordinary folks with a peculiarly average boy with a penchant for art. Telly could remember his first conversation with the couple in the local supermarket, when their carts collided into each other in the middle of aisle nine.

Mr. and Mrs. Rye both had pale streaks of what resembled plaster in their hair, though at the time they were only in their late thirties. You could easily tell from their appearances that they were very rich. Mr.

Rye's included a pair of high-end glasses that contrasted heavily to the tarnished lenses most wore, and Mrs. Rye's skirt was so well stitched it must have been expensive. This did not draw Telly's attention to them, as most everyone in town spared their money toward smaller things. Their faces were roughened as if they spent years in the harsh cold, and both had large noses with small nostrils; they could have very well been siblings rather than married. Mrs. and Mr. Rye had brown eyes, but Mrs. Rye's were paler. It was the one feature that their son shared, and it was the feature that caught Telly's attention in the grocery store, before his cart collided with theirs, of course.

Her eye color matched exactly a shade of paint he was desperately looking for, and he was still latched onto them through the impact of the carts smashing together that made an unconscious apology come from his mouth.

"I'm sorry about that," said Telly as he watched Mrs. Rye check if her milk carton was crushed. She looked up at Telly and smiled, showing two strands of teeth that completed the happiness in the eyes.

"I wasn't looking where I was going," he said.

"That's alright. We've got nowhere to be," Mrs. Rye said, her husband smiling at her comment.

Telly felt slightly uncomfortable at the free share of information.

"I doubt our son even knows we've left the house," giggled Mr. Rye. His voice was surprisingly mischievous, like one of a child's.

"He just sits outside all day. Doesn't fool around or anything. He's got friends asking him to go places but he never goes. He's a *gloomy* guy."

Telly adjusted his cart and, because it looked like the couple was waiting for an answer, asked them how old their boy was.

He was sixteen, weeks short of seventeen. Besides being a rather melrose man, their son was recently expelled from school in a neighboring state, prompting a transfer here. His hobbies really did only include, from Telly's current knowledge, sitting around or working.

"Maybe something's got him down," said Telly. "Have they got *any* flour left?" He busied himself looking through the shelves, but he could feel the couple's presence still near. Then he looked up and realized they were sorting through the shelves as well, looking for flour. They were trying to help him. Telly's useless little heart teemed with sudden affection for this odd duo he did not know.

"He's an artist, my son. Very talented. That's his only interest," Mr. Rye mentioned.

Telly stopped his searching. "Artist, you say?"

6.

Something indeed did have Mckenzie down and Telly heard it over the phone the next Tuesday.

"I've got to skip our lesson tomorrow," he said.

"Do you really?"'

"Yes, yes. I'm busier after school, that's all."

"You're busier after school *all* the time?"

"No, just this one day, I believe."

Telly could hear Mr. and Mrs. Linton in the background, which was odd, for Mr. Linton usually worked later hours. Perhaps someone had died.

"Has someone died?" asked Telly.

"No. You think because I can't have our lesson tomorrow that somebody died?"

"You're speaking in a funeral parlor voice."

I can tell you myself that nobody had died, although I can say that the existence of Mckenzie's odd front was noticeable. His voice was hushed and had a low tone, like Telly's tutoring of him had been paid by a mischievous relative instead of Mckenzie's parents. Perhaps he was in trouble.

"Are you in trouble?" asked Telly.

"No. What do you mean by trouble?"

"With your parents, I presume. I'm already under the acknowledgement that they do not care for me as well as I have wished. Has my secret agenda of corrupting you sent them over the edge?"

"I just can't have it tomorrow."

"Alright."

"Asking all those questions was a bit unprofessional. What if somebody had died?"

"Then I would have offered my sincere condolences."

He hung up.

Telly happened to spy his suspicious student milling around town that Saturday. He had been surrounded by boys at the town hall. A group of them. All most likely eighteen. He knew they had to be at least legal and he pinpointed that age specifically, noting the way the boys nudged one another with childlike playfulness, then reverted back to their standard expression of working long hours. Telly considered saying hello, then chose against it. He had never seen Mckenzie with friends before.

In the afternoon of that Saturday, Telly took to his living room, after completing all necessary responsibilities of adulthood, and looked at his canvas. It was blank. Fucking thing was empty. What on Earth, he thought, are you supposed to paint on a blank canvas? He thought back to his last session with Mckenzie, who went into detailed descriptions of his imagined painting before putting it down. He would describe every line the brush made, every human error was included, each color was strategic, just like Telly had taught him. Mckenzie's beginning canvases, however white, were never empty. He could see the image before it fell into his mind. Telly painted his canvas white, then another layer of white, and another, until it was too white for any colors to show. He never said it, but his paintings took longer to think of than complete. Artist-block was normal.

In the evening of that Saturday, Telly found it in the mail. It was a party invitation, to which party he did not know of. He read the nice, neat lettering on the front and took the invite inside. He left it on his kitchen counter and ignored the address line. He was already familiar with the place. He took off his nice dress shoes he had had on to teach, took off his tie, contemplated cleaning his entire house. The whole lot of it was so very undisturbed, unlived in, that he had a temptation of greasing the windows. They were far too big. Telly had always felt small looking out at them. He denied this request of his brain, instead cooking himself a piece of chicken and nothing else. He burnt the edges of the meat so that the beige color curled inwards toward its stomach, black crimping the sides and bottom, so that it cracked, hot and electric, on your tongue, and the black powdered his dinner plate. Char was an offering to the gods.

At ten o'clock, for Telly had not much else to do, he sat on the floor in front of his painting. The one that had yet to be painted. His palette of colors was yet to dry, so opportunity was still available, and yet, Telly could not fathom dipping a brush into yellow, or blue or green or gray or red, taking his hand and outlining a picture that he could not see nor describe perfectly clear out loud. He felt a sort of sickness in his head, a mind boggling, widespread disease that cut off his ears and fingertips, so that he felt the blood pumping but unable to get where it needed. His eyes were too bright for his being, and he watched his talent slip away from his carved hands and fall into the soles of his shoes, where he could crease it into the ground. His talent was one of a mute belter; there was no better way to be belittled.

And yet, Mckenzie had what Telly did not. There was music in his hands and ears and mouth. He lived with each touch of paint just a bit longer, and there was no sense of mistakes, even if he had gone outside of the lines. Telly could have watched him for hours, and in his thoughts, he painted Mckenzie a glaring green, pushed him into the water and knelt on his chest, snarled and bit and fought the passive assailant and his paint-stained hold. Telly pictured his talent leaking into the water with himself standing over as victor, pumping his fists, until seeing that his own body was no longer physical, that he was merely the point between A and B, and he had become the kind of color that is given no name, besides Nothing.

Telly thought back to the party invitation, the blandness of the colors and the little emotions stirred at the words. It was a paper of Nothing, yet he could not let go of seeing its image in his head. During his initial walk through the door earlier that day, he had dropped it on the counter, and there it sat until ten, and at ten he pictured the invite sitting there for decades, the paper yellowing to pulp and the words so narrowed they lost all meaning. The moon was out, its silver blade cutting through the curtains and layering over the hardwood floor of Telly's flat. The light touched his toes. Remains of the day were trickling through, and Telly considered walking to the kitchen, finding the counter where he had dropped the party invitation, and looking at it again. Maybe if he looked twice, the real meaning behind such a party wouldn't be obvious anymore. Maybe the "18th Birthday" would hide all of it from his eyes. For the invite was not for a birthday party. It was for a goodbye party.

—

Telly, truly, had not seen a cake in a very long while.

It was an expectation of war, I understand. There were families collecting money, giving it up in plainly American efforts, and nobody had the time for a cake. Birthdays came and passed, and there were small presents and hugs. Your celebration included your father sitting in the living room smoking a cigar and listening to the radio. Birthdays came and passed. War did not.

Even in his own town, where expectations of American effort were never expressed, cake was not seen. There were few celebrations of a large gathering. The bakeries had small cupcakes hard as rock and everything was so very lukewarm that the coldest of weather never froze the ponds, and the town meetings never encouraged a raised voice. Telly had never thought of it before, but perhaps it was his town's solemn prayers for a quick end.

A week later, Telly dressed smartly, but not uptight, and drove himself to Mckenzie's house, a place he had never seen at night. At 5:30, the white paint brightened the leering trees, and the glow of the light inside was warm. He ignored the balloons ceremonially tied to the mailbox. He knocked on the front door.

It opened fast. "Hi, Telly. How are you now?" said Mrs. Rye. She was wearing her best jewelry, Telly noted.

"Swell. How are you?"

Mrs. Rye let Telly inside, pointed toward the living room and kitchen, where a small number of people had gathered. Telly spotted Mckenzie immediately. He braced for the goodbye.

A pretty house they have as well, I thought. It was not the nicest on the block, but it was bigger than those in neighboring areas, a living, breathing house opposed to Telly's empty one. Mckenzie's mother, after bringing Telly to the main event, had taken to arranging an assortment of appetizers on the kitchen table, although no one was very hungry. At first glance, you would have thought she was crying. However, I chalk it up to the glint of the dishes rather than an overwhelming urge to please her son.

He was sitting in a chair in the corner of the kitchen and finding that being in a corner did not immediately exclude you from a scene. He thought back to the planning of this party, when he sat with his mother one morning and, in a burst of energy, decided who he'd invite. Several of Mckenzie's school friends were gathered together talking. They looked as though they were enjoying themselves. No harm toward them, Mckenzie thought. But Mckenzie was already wishing that this party had not taken place, and maybe wishing that there was no need for it.

An hour in, Mckenzie had made small talk with each guest sufficiently to where his father clapped his shoulder and smiled wide, the kind of smile that many children are able to understand. Go have fun, it says. To the best of his ability, he tried. But an hour in, he was still sitting alone. If you did not count Telly, that was.

Telly was standing next to him silently, eating his slice of (bittersweet, chocolate) cake very weirdly, he noted. He would stab his cake with the fork, then eat off the frosting and let the dry cake crumble back onto his plate. He was the only man of his age attending and perhaps a matter of interest to the other partygoers. His black hair and eyes and crooked smile made him sound monochrome by description, but to Mckenzie he seemed like a strange comic book character, one generally positioned behind a weapon in a cap. He was also the only member of the party not bursting with joy or sadness or nostalgia or drunkenness, which made him the strangest character of all. I imagined war would look good on him.

Telly looked down at Mckenzie with his mouth still full. "What're you looking at?"

"Nothing, you just eat funny."

"That is somehow extremely insulting, thanks."

"I just noticed."

"I have a refined palette, thank you. Why aren't you eating any cake? It's your favorite."

"My mom thinks I'm too young," said Mckenzie.

"For cake?"

"No. Adulthood. Bills, kids, you know."

"Well, nobody's too young for bills, my friend. Besides, *I* think you're too old."

"For what?"

Telly grinned, that crooked mouth lifting. "I think you're too old to say 'taxes' and 'kids' the way you do. Future reality is hovering right over us, so get that bitter sound out of your voice."

"What about you?" Mckenzie said bluntly.

"What about me?"

"You're twenty-six. You've got no wife or children. Do you even pay your bills? And you act like you know everything in the world that is worth knowing."

"Maybe I do."

"You don't. How do you even make money? Being my tutor cannot be your only source of income."

"I'm a course teacher. I do lectures at the community college."

"You're not making much cash from that," said Mckenzie.

"You sound really sure about that. But, no, I am not."

"How do you stay on your feet?"

Telly gave a tittered chuckle with no amusement. "I have the fortune of blood relations to folks who spent too much of my childhood in labor. They're pretty well off, as I am. They don't interest me, if you can comprehend that, and I, them."

"Why?" asked Mckenzie. "If you don't mind saying, I mean."

He sighed and wiggled the corner of his mouth up. "This war brought a lot of people closer together and some it pushed farther away. And you see no one is really immune to hate."

"Oh." It hadn't answered Mckenzie's questions, but he let it go.

"You know, when I go out of town, I get weird looks. By strangers."

"Why?"

"Well, I'm very blatantly Tuscan, or perhaps people see me as another type of foreigner, I don't know. But my guess is because I'm Tuscan and there's been some trouble there. You wouldn't hear about it in this town."

"What kind of trouble?"

"Italy had its role in this war," he said simply. "A very complicated one, mind you."

Mckenzie did not have questions at that.

"Can I ask you more," he asked instead, "if you'd like me to learn about adulthood?"

"Knock yourself out."

"Why aren't you married?" said Mckenzie curiously, and he creased his eyebrows at Telly's winning grin.

"Well, I'm afraid my wife would kill me."

"Seriously?"

"I'm not the man a woman would like to be bothered by. Also, I think I would be a very killable man. Go get married yourself, find some girl to be with and you'll see where I come from."

Mckenzie nodded, not recognizing that Telly hoped for him to laugh, and observed his party. His father was having a lively, yet civil debate with some colleagues, and his face was beginning to glow pleasantly from the alcohol. He just noticed that several guests had filtered out the door and that he had not said goodbye. His school friends had already gone and Mckenzie found that he did not care very much.

"Alright then. My turn."

"What?" Mckenzie turned back toward his tutor, whom he suddenly realized did not seem to be much of a tutor to him. Possibly more like a lazy friend who happened to critique your work.

"I am asking the questions now."

"You already know a lot about me. What more do you need? It's different when I ask. It's like I am interviewing you for your application as a tutor."

"You have the right to completely ignore these questions I throw at you, then."

"No, no. I'll answer."

"Alright. Well, happy birthday."

"That's not a question."

"I think it needs to be said. I barely feel as though I am attending a birthday party at the moment." Telly smiled and it did not go away at Mckenzie's unhappy expression.

"You didn't need to come."

"Hold there," he said. "I wanted to. I won't see you again for a while, you know. When do you leave?"

"What're you talking about?"

"Quit with the bullshit, alright? I saw the invitation, okay, I knew this party wasn't for your birthday. You don't even like birthdays; you told me this. Why else would you be having a *party*, Mckenzie?" Telly's voice had lowered and his usual pretentious tone was gone. Mckenzie noticed, strangely, at this moment, that Telly almost sounded like everyone else.

"Did my mother tell you?" he said gingerly.

"No, God, your mother didn't tell me. I figured it out myself," Telly uttered, each word more heavily pronounced than the last. "You know, Mckenzie, you could have told me. I would've had some more time finding a new student."

Mckenzie looked up. His brain was working too slowly. "Are you kidding?"

"Are you?"

"I have to go, Telly. I already chose to go."

"You didn't have to go, that's the thing!" Telly said and audibly sucked in a breath through his teeth. "We've got a lot of privilege living here, Mckenzie. Many people would kill to be here, in your position."

"I didn't ask to be here. And if I leave, then maybe someone can take my spot."

"Okay, Mckenzie. Funny. You wanna go and kill people? Go and do it. Just remember, it doesn't matter who they are, you just shoot and shoot and try not to be a fucking idiot."

Mckenzie gave a slight, humorless laugh. Then it dropped from his face. "Are you upset with me? Genuinely?"

Telly had the nerve to look surprised, all tenseness washing away from his face. "Of course not."

"Ok. Because you don't really have a right to be."

Telly's eyes creased and wrinkled at the corner. "I'm not upset with you."

Telly suddenly realized he was still holding his plate of cake and put it on a nearby table and turned back to his friend. He shrugged. "I should be going now." He did not give a reason for his departure. He smoothed his finger over the scar under his eyebrow and Mckenzie suddenly wondered where he had gotten it, and why he had not asked before.

"Ok," said Mckenzie. He took Telly's hand and shook it, then let go very quickly.

"Good luck, Mckenzie," said Telly. "And tell your parents thank you for me."

"I will," he said.

Telly nodded and followed the steps back into the house. Mckenzie watched him until he vanished out the front door, and he was left alone at his eighteenth birthday party, at eight o'clock in early March. It was the last time they would ever see each other.

7.

She was four years younger than him, and he fixed the type of cars she had always admired, the ones she saw in magazines, the sheer slippery ones she would find in his drawers. She knew a lot about her brother, despite being four years younger, and it was never any information he gave to her.

She was eleven in 1941, December, and he was fifteen. Many days, their parents sent them out on errands to do with the scrapped money of the week. They had been doing this since she was five. It was a Saturday tradition.

She walked beside him and he, a quiet fellow, beside her. They were both rather silent. If she asked him why he had gone dull, he would tell her that there was nothing to say. And he was always very true about that.

She would window shop down the streets of Boston and try to ignore the beggars. Sometimes they pulled at the hem of her dress, which took her mother too little stitches to create, or tapped her brother's shoes. However, she liked these errands. She liked to feel the weight of the weather full on her face, the bright sun casting a dim glow, or the brilliant slap of cold biting her eyes. I understood that she liked to feel her brother's presence because many days, on days other than Saturday, she could not feel him at all.

Her brother often told her that they were better off than some. He would point at the sidewalk folks and tell her that they had run out of luck. Luck, he said, was hard to find. We aren't too poor, he said, but we're not rich. We do, he said. She believed him on everything he said about the topic. She knew he had friends who were too poor, and not very rich at all.

In December of 1941, they walked together one Saturday down the streets of Boston. Lately, she noted, her brother had taken to reading the paper on such errands. She would find him at the dinner table with his eyes down and she would look to see the words beside his chili. He hated chili, too. They had it three times a week. Then he would excuse himself and go to the dealership. He spent his time after school there, oiling whatever, and when she greeted him as he opened the front door, he waved her off. He smelled of oil.

"Stop it," she said this Saturday. He looked up at her.

"What?"

"You are reading the paper. Knock it off."

"I am staying informed."

"The whole country is too informed."

"That's an opinion I really disagree on. No. No, actually. You're right." He folded his paper. "I'll stop reading."

By 1942, their parents had stopped requesting such errands from them, and Saturdays were suddenly free. She never knew why there was suddenly no need for the errands, but she noticed her winter clothing was fuller, longer baths were allowed, and chili was not served three times a week. On her brother's birthday, they had a real celebration, the first one she could truly remember. It became her favorite memory, her brother smiling at the little gifts he was given, his friends mussing his hair. She loved her brother's birthday.

At the very end of February, 1945, her sorrows of missing errands had gone, and she was fifteen. It was late that night and she sat in the living room with her mother and father, her brother, and watched the Lottery. The ball rolled down the slot. Her brother was nineteen.

When they called it, she did not think of him. She thought of his birthday party. Her favorite memory of all her years. It could not even be called a party in her head anymore. Now it was just a sentence.

8.

I was at the loading station the day Mckenzie had packed to leave on, and it was one of few days where I had seen that number of boys. They had all packed their belongings and their dog tags, memorized their numbers over the previous week, some the night before, some a month in advance. Some had been patiently waiting; some were too patient. Mckenzie fell somewhere in between.

"Goodbye," he said as fast as he could. The sight of the bus before him was eerie, the sickening color like the children's books in a doctor's office, the smell of clementines. It burnt my invisible eyes.

"Wait, now," said his mother. His mother with her pale moon eyes and her perked nostrils. "Do you have everything you need? God, I barely know what you need."

"Yes, yes, yes. Yes to all the questions," he said.

"But I only asked one!"

"Mckenzie." His father, the mellow man, bent his weathered face toward his. The bus gave a trembling grunt behind them, and he twisted so he was no longer facing it. "You'll do great."

"It's not a talent show, Dad."

"I know, I know. But you'll do alright, okay?"

"Alright. I'll see you soon."

"Soon, yes!" his father muttered distractedly, running a hand over his face. "Yes, soon. See you soon. Get some leave."

"We love you," his mother added.

Mckenzie said the required reassuring words of a leaving boy, did the required actions to complete his goodbye. He found that he had never meant any words or touches as much as he did then. He tried his best to photograph their faces, so they would be bled into his memory with ink forever. He tried not to look back.

There were many seats open at the back of the bus. So Mckenzie got on, waving slightly through the windows as he walked down the aisle. He counted six boys on the vehicle, all seated alone. Mckenzie sat four seats from the very last row, surrounded by empty spots. He felt as though he was placed in someone else's little pool of misery, someone who had not yet gotten aboard. He felt numb and stupid and could not comprehend what he had just left behind.

In minutes, the bus filled and shook as the driver started it up. Mckenzie was still sitting alone between several rambunctious boys who seemed to know one another. The rest of the group was fairly quiet. I watched as the bus departed the loading station, watched each boy wave out the window, and I waved back.

It was ten minutes into the ride surrounded by fourteen other boys from God-knows-where that he began to panic.

Several boys from the back were playing a strange game where they punched each other's arms repeatedly. There was one in the front with his head buried into his bag, and some seemed to know one another. Neither appealed to Mckenzie in the way of friendship very much. So he stayed silent in his seat, thinking about how soon the group of fourteen boys would be almost indistinguishable from each other. He chewed the inside of his cheek and stared out the window at the landscape blurring together. Then there was a loud voice in his ear.

"Hey, boy," said John St. Dennis. "Does your face hurt?"

Mckenzie spun around to look at the boy who spoke to him. His jaw was terribly triangular and strong, brown hair horribly thin and sculpted over his forehead with gel. His face was one of frenzied laughter, and although he was ugly, he was attractive.

"What?"

"I said, does your face hur*t*?" John emphasized his *t*'s, grinning. Behind him in another seat, an intensely red-headed boy was bright faced trying not to laugh, and the boy sitting beside John was looking bored, his black framed glasses high on his nose.

"Why, should it?" Mckenzie asked the boy. He frowned in response, and the smile on the redhead faded away. The boy in the glasses nodded like he was not surprised at Mckenzie's answer.

"I told you, John," said glasses boy dully. "I told you he wouldn't give you a straight answer. He's got a shifty look. Too smart for you."

John laughed with well-intended laughter, a sound that almost made Mckenzie smile. He decided then that he liked this John very much. He reminded him of someone. Something was there that he just couldn't put his finger on.

"Well, it's a joke, you see," John explained.

"I got that," said Mckenzie.

"Well, I'm supposed to say 'does your face hurt?', you respond with 'no,' and I complete the joke with—"

"Because it's killing me."

"How'd you know my joke?" John's tan forehead crinkled in confusion.

The redhead behind him piped up, "Maybe he's a mind reader. Like Harry Houdini."

"Oh, don't be stupid," said John. He exaggeratedly examined Mckenzie, looking him up and down and narrowing his eyes. Then he pouted again. "I try that joke on a lot of guys. I think it's a clever invention of mine, don't you?"

"Harry Houdini's not a mind reader," added Lee Collins, the glasses boy. The redhead turned away from John looking slightly hurt and began talking to the boys playing a card game.

"You didn't make the joke. I've heard it before," said Mckenzie.

John sighed, genuinely distraught. "Fuck, I thought I created something great. I thought it was genius of me, too." He straightened up a bit more in his seat, nudged Lee Collins, then asked, "D'you know the string trick?"

"The string trick?"

"Yeah, you put the imaginary string through one ear and pull it out the other ear and it goes through your brain."

"Oh."

"Should I try it on you?"

"No, I mean, I know that one. I'm not fucking stupid," said Mckenzie. And he smiled for the first time on that bus. "I'm Mckenzie."

"My God, what a name." John groaned and stretched his hand over the seat for him to shake. "I'm John St. Dennis."

"Lee Collins. We're from Boston," said the glasses boy, who shook Mckenzie's hand as well.

"Where're you from, bucky boy?" John said, resting his head on the back of Mckenzie's seat.

"You first."

"I'm from Boston too, s'how I know Lee." He grinned vivaciously. "Now Mr. Micky or whatever."

Mckenzie told the boys where he was from, and he watched the playful expressions on their faces drop. It was an expression he had seen numerous times from the people who understood the town name. John sniffed. Lee nodded. "So you don't have to be here. You weren't drafted."

"Were you?"

"Maybe," said Lee. "I signed up some time back. I didn't tell anyone. And I didn't get called in until they rang my birthday. I think they accidentally erased my name from the list. If that's how it works. I don't really know."

"What about you?"

John sighed again. "Drafted. My dad threw a fucking fit when I came home with the news. He didn't want me to go." There was a moment of silence, then John spoke up again. "I'm not complaining. I wanna be with Lee anywho, so. *Tis an honor!*"

"I know," said Mckenzie.

The ride was fairly enjoyable, Mckenzie thought, watching the two boys interact, the way the shapes and colors and ideas coming from their mouths sounded so dissimilar, yet exactly the same. Halfway to their destination, the boys pulled out their lunches. John ate bent over with a wide grimace and very fast; Lee sat upright, taking a longer time and staring out a window. They were all on their way to a stranger who

knew their names, without the stories behind them, and Mckenzie would watch the two boys seated behind him talk many times, until the course of our story departs.

9.

"*B-29s burn* Japs' sixth city," said Carrie, as Rico opened the door for Telly. She had Ines balanced on her hip and Donna tapping her knee.

"What's that?" asked Rico. He hung up Telly's jacket. Telly frowned.

"B-29s burn Japs' sixth city. It's in the papers outside here. My mother called; she just told me."

"B-29s? What the hell's that?"

"A bomber plane. American one, mostly," said Telly. He accepted a cup of coffee from Carrie and sat on their sofa.

Rico sat beside him, his wife in the armchair across. "Now, how do you know of that, Tel?"

"I built planes," he said simply. "What have those things done?"

"She just said," Rico said. "They burnt the Japs' sixth city."

"That's what my mother said. She forgets we don't get the same papers down here."

"Is that a lot of good or what?"

"I don't know." She sighed, crossed her legs, and smiled at the bobbing heads of her two girls playing by her feet. "It's front headlines. It must be. My mother sounded excited."

"Good news for us then."

"Yes, it must." Carrie's voice trailed off, and as she studied the floor, a tiny crease appeared between her brows. "Some man calls the German soldiers disillusioned."

"What, in the paper?"

"Yes. He says something about doughboys. I don't know about that."

"Isn't Germany still in the fight?" asked Telly, leaning forward toward Carrie. He couldn't understand his sudden interest.

"Yes," continued Carrie. "That's what makes it so strange, apparently. The same man in the paper, he wrote about some psychological study. About why they keep fighting when defeat is inevitable."

"So, defeat is inevitable for Germany?"

"That's what everyone is saying."

"Well, that makes no sense," Telly said irritably, his face narrowed. "Why do they keep fighting then? If defeat is inevitable?"

"Ingrained German obedience. And fear of a nameless future."

"Oh."

"Among other things, my mother said."

Telly sipped his coffee. It was always scalding at Carrie's house. That was how he enjoyed it.

"I think Mckenzie's going to Germany," he said.

Rico looked concerned. Carrie just smiled softly.

"He's not going to Germany," she said, and smiled again.

"You don't know that."

"Telly," she said. She stood up from her chair. Took his coffee from his hands. The mug was nearly empty. "He's not going to Germany. Let me get you another coffee."

He watched Carrie walk to the kitchen, holding his mug. He tried to recall the moment when he swallowed an entire mug of hot coffee and forgot about it.

"Hey there, Frank."

Telly looked to see his godson grinning up at him and his father. His throat felt suddenly very, very burnt, and he was grateful when all Carrie brought back for him was water.

10.

Travers, the lagging fellow, was ready to meet his new party. The boys had seen his name on papers and such, and he theirs, but he had never met them before. He felt dread.

Sergeant Travers was tall and strong-looking and this look about him was deemed respectable. He was not too brawny to be outrageously frightening, but his arms were powerful enough to keep troops in shape if he had to. His hands were whittled from cracking. He smoked pipe tobacco and it didn't show; his teeth were not yellow and his breath was not terrible. That finely buzzed blonde hair of his was thin enough to spy his scalp and see the nicks the razor had done. And his eyes were too blue for a war, and I saw once, so very clearly, that they flickered like a closet light bulb. He had begun cracking his knuckles at the start of the war and swore he would not stop such a habit until it was over. He drank single malt whiskey, disliked paperwork and those who worked above him. He mindlessly entertained himself by sitting in his office fidgeting with the buttons on his uniform, fidgeting with the curtains that let the sun draw into the room, fidgeting with his bronze star that he tended to keep in a drawer and was tarnished from the wooden floors of his private space. Do not mistake this for anger; the award was thrown coming from a man of despondency. His nails were cut with a pocketknife, his knuckles were too sharp against his skin, and he smoked out the back window of his office, so as not to bother anyone with the fumes. Three photographs sat on his desk, one of his young daughter and wife, one of his young mother, and the last of a squad he had trained the previous year. Where they had gone, if they were rising in ranks or they were falling, he didn't want to know.

I once observed him walking through the courtyards smoking and whistling. I saw him hold the hand of a dying soldier, a man that was trampled somehow, while Travers thought of how he held the hand of his dying mother once. And he only whistled when he was alone.

Sergeant was terrible with names, but the boys already knew that when they were taken off the bus, brought to camp, and shown the entrance to the cabin where they heard him humming "The Sound of Music," specifically the part where the hills are alive. His fingers in his pocket fingered a rogue cigar from an hour before, when he sat in front of his office window making jokes to associate with the names of his new crew. Sergeant Travers was God-awful with names, would be considerably worse from the number of extra men in his squad, and that became very much apparent when his whistling stopped abruptly and he gave "St. Douglas" the first order.

"Sir?" wondered John St. Dennis, whom the sergeant was looking at, aloud.

"You heard me, St. Douglas, shut the door behind you."

"Oh, sir," John sighed with relief. "It's St. Dennis."

"My sorries, St. Douglas. Shut the door," Sergeant Travers dryly mumbled.

They had turned in their civilian clothes and their belongings, and they were wearing those standard issue uniforms. The skinniest of the group, the black-haired boy, wore one far too small; the biggest boy, the married one, had a uniform too big. You could see the scalps on each guy, and Mckenzie wondered if they were repeating their own unique number in their heads just as he was. John moved first. He dropped his small leftover bag on a chosen bed, the closest bed to the door. The others moved just as he did. They did not unpack.

Mckenzie noticed that in the parallel rows of fourteen beds that there was an extra spot. He counted the group again. Thirteen boys, including himself. He was forcibly reminded of the time he was invited to a boy's party, in grade school, where there were more than ten boys sleeping over and Mckenzie had spoken to none of them.

"Line," said Sergeant, "I want a line."

This is it, thought Mckenzie. This is when he yells at us and makes us cry. But, nevertheless, the boys lined up, each standing in front of their chosen beds, facing the others parallel. He could not help wondering if it was the correct form of line.

John and a heavy-jawed and armed man were facing one another closest to the sergeant. He focused his attention first on the unknown boy.

"Alright, what's your name, soldier?" he spoke uncomfortably loud, but without the fury behind yelling.

"Sid Dorman, Sergeant."

Sid Dorman was the first with a name.

"And where are you from, soldier?"

He told the group. Travers looked at the boy beside Dorman. He stepped in front of him next, the boy with black bangs, the kind that hung like curtains. No one had noticed at the time, but he had stolen John St. Dennis' socks from his bag on the bus.

"Mike Stroshine, Sergeant," the boy said very fast, before Travers could say anything to him.

"And are you supposed to be here, soldier?" Sergeant said curiously in response.

Mike creased his eyebrows together and the corners of his mouth turned down. "Believe so, Sergeant."

"You don't sound too sure."

"I am."

"Then, alright. I'll let you by." He turned to the others and waved his hands. "Sneak."

Next in line, Mckenzie recognized, was the boy who had had his face hidden in his bag during the ride. He was very pale, almost sickly, and young, Mckenzie noticed. He wasn't aware that, at the time, he was actually twenty-one.

"Your name, soldier?"

The man in question sniffed, his lucid unnerving eyes unable to meet his questioner. "Kenneth Green, sir."

"Sir is a new one. Gimme your age." Greene looked up in slight shock. "C'mon, now." Sergeant snapped twice in a row.

"Twenty-one."

"Now, slow down. Be sure now." At that, a few boys let out soft cries of laughter.

The redhead with the nasal voice who seemed to know John and Lee stood next to Kenneth.

"Name?"

"Joe Marshall, Sergeant."

"You get on the wrong bus?"

"No, Sergeant."

"Well, you're kinda puny. Sure you got the right place?"

"Yes, Sergeant."

"Hm." Sergeant studied Marshall a bit, squinting his eyes.

John was smiling.

"You." Lee was the next one to be interrogated. He stood tall, without the vapidness Mike had.

"Lee Collins, Sergeant." He gave a slight nod with his face void of expression. Travers smiled unexpectedly. He had the sort of nice smile that they boys would have never expected.

"My daughter's name is Leanna," Travers said, nodding. "We call her Lee."

Lee didn't say anything. He just nodded again. He never really said much with any expression. But if someone asked John, which many people did, he said it was just the Lee way.

"You're William White," said Travers, pointing to the boy beside Lee.

"Yes, Sergeant."

"Oh, no kidding. You've got the blondest goddamn hair I've ever seen. That's white."

William White smiled. "I'm Fritz's favorite lover," was all he said. Some of the boys even laughed. It wasn't very funny.

"Okay, White, now shut the fuck up."

He did, unashamedly and likeably, as though he had expected the order.

"Jesus, Mary, and Joseph." Travers nodded to the boy who was directly to Mckenzie's left. "I've really got the little ones."

"Forrest Burns," the boy said. He was extraordinarily tall and skinny, like a stick figure drawing.

"I think I could *snap* you in half," called out Travers.

"I'm fast, Sergeant."

"Are you now? Good for you, boy. Hope that helps you with the big man up there." And then he looked at Mckenzie, whose stomach felt funny in a way where he knew it was not nerves or sickness, but possibly his intestines twisting together to make a noose.

"Two shrimpy kids in a row. Goddamn my luck."

Mckenzie opted to nod and say nothing. Travers' eyes were terribly piercing, like pressing your fingertips into snow, and he realized, his thoughts strangely full of clarity, that he would not have been able to speak anyhow.

"Mckenzie Rye."

"Yes, Sergeant," he said. Pride was rising in his chest at how normal the words had sounded out loud.

"Thanks for confirming your name, boy. Eat some fucking food."

The tension dropped and Mckenzie noticed the other boys grinning, the ones whose names had already been called. He suddenly found the situation amusing and turned with vindictive excitement to the last few uncalled boys. Sergeant frowned, raking a hand over his close-cut hair, as he took in the two boys standing next in line.

"Okay, now don't tell me. You two are the twins."

"Yes, Sergeant," said the one on Mckenzie's side. After months of studying the two, Mckenzie would see that Vicky, the twin who spoke first, was the tanner one, and the one less likely to knock his teeth out.

"Vicky."

"Yes."

"You're Albert."

"Al."

"Alright, Al. What the fuck kind of lab created you?"

He was correct in asking that sort of question, Mckenzie thought. The two looked exactly the same, the same skin and sandy hair. However, there was no answer from the twins except a smile from Vicky, so Travers moved on.

"Jack Betchel, Sergeant," said Betchel, the most muscular of the lot and who had intelligent, calming eyes.

"You're married, Jack?" asked Sergeant.

"Yes, I am, Sergeant." He wore a wedding band on his finger.

"Well, get back home before dinner time."

"Will do, Sergeant."

John was next. When Travers spotted him, he laughed aloud and said, "Why, it's St. Douglas!" John grinned widely, and the boys smiled along with his relaxed expression.

"Yes, Sergeant, good to meet you."

"Never gotten that before."

"I meant it, Sergeant," said John, but Mckenzie noticed he said it lightly.

"Well, then, you've lost your mind, St. Douglas." And Travers turned to the last one of the group uncalled for.

"Sammy Brenner, Sergeant," said the blonde-haired, sly-eyed boy. His shoulders were taut, muscles pulled tight.

"Yes, yes, Brenner. Another Aryan youth."

"It's a curse, Sergeant," said Brenner, and he wasn't laughing. None of the boys were laughing.

"It is, Brenner."

And with that, Travers turned to the group, waved his hands wildly, and said, "Your dinner's being served soon. Unpack your shit."

Uniformly, the group moved to their beds and piled out of their belongings. Travers stopped at the door. He looked them over. "Oh."

Sid Dorman straightened, and the group followed his gaze and fell quiet.

"Good day. Go eat some fucking food."

April.

2

It was April first. It was the last thirty days of a global chess game that had begun a nightmare ago, and the king and queen, balancing on black and white, would soon retire to their tower and never come out. This, we understood, was inevitable. We waited for it. We were poised by the radios with our cigars poised at our teeth and the words poised on our tongues, everything frozen in time, like the movements of a ballerina, one waiting for her cue, when she leaps in the air and discovers she cannot fly.

Life, inevitably, continued. March was cloudy and senseless; this we had expected. The first rain of April, in the hometown which this odyssey revolves, was met with layers of sodden tar. The roads were refurbished. The flowers gleamed. The air stunk of a second grader's recess, and I watched as the bombs and the planes and the smoke and the fire, the twisted shrapnel in someone's brother's leg, the bloodied uniform skirt of someone's mother, never touched the newly paved roads. They were picture perfect.

The papers were tiring, however. I can only imagine the number of town newspaper layoffs that year, for there was hardly anything to write about. Their honored citizens had left a while ago, and now, there were only the opened shops and the heated papers, so fresh that the ink could have borne into your fingerprints, or the occasional storyline of a lost dog, or an elderly neighbor who waved goodbye to the school children. But alas, no matter the layoffs in journalism, the writers still did not take their free time to read the works of those busy on the frontlines.

Many days, the thoughts of Carrie Romano went through my head. Every day now, there were more boys outside the town hall, whispering. And they were *boys*. I once witnessed one, no older than fifteen, attempt to nudge his way inside with the others, until the older boys pushed him back. I watched as he waited on the steps of the building until the elders came out. They later played baseball on an empty field. I wanted to hand their lost ball back to them.

Telly woke up on April first and truly believed that March had created another fucking day. It was a long month. He went to his bathroom, stretched out his legs, brushed his teeth on the toilet, and shaved. He studied his face in the mirror. Telly had never really noticed it before, or maybe never thought of it, but he looked as Italian as an Italian could get. He had the typical Roman nose; centered perfectly in the middle of his face; his eyebrows were dark and in fine shape, pointed downwards at the tips; his eyes were dark; and he had a twisted bow mouth. His skin was lighter than his parents, and he would never be as good a cook as his mother, nor a well off businessman like his father. He thought of his parents as he looked in the mirror, and thought of last week, when he had gone out of town for errands, and a woman called him something strange. An enemy alien. An enemy of what, he did not know, and unfortunately for Telly, he happened to be from the same planet as everyone else.

"Jesus Christ," he said out loud, as if that was who was looking at him from the mirror, but he was merely reacting to the ringing of the telephone. Nobody called much lately. He had not spoken to Rico in two weeks—or was it three?

Telly, dressed still in pajamas, picked up the phone where it was sitting uselessly on his kitchen table. "Hello?"

"Hello?"

"Yeah?"

"Hello?"

"Hi," said Telly. "Who the hell is this?"

"It's Anita."

"Jesus Christ," he said aloud. He'd really summoned a demon now. "Ma, what's the matter? Put Dad on." That was the other thing about Telly's mother. She referred to herself as "Anita," as though Telly had another mother and she needed to specify.

"You're at church?" said Anita. "I'll put your father on."

"Yeah, yeah, okay, put Dad on, Ma."

There was some shuffling. "Clau, it's your son."

"I'll take it."

"Hey, Dad?"

"Albertelli."

"Yeah, Dad. What's going on? I have to get to work."

"Did you call us? What is the issue?"

Telly groaned. "Ma called me, Dad. What's going on?"

"Your mother says you are at church?"

"No, no. Why'd you call?"

"Arnaldo is in the hospital. He wants to see you."

First, he frowned. The strangest form of nostalgia overcame him, although he was hearing of a memory soon to end. "Arnie Giovanni?" he asked, though he understood the answer.

"Yes, yes. Arnie. He is in the hospital. He wishes to see you."

"Dad, he's dying?"

There was a small silence. "Yes, Albertelli, I believe so. I will give you the address."

He gave the address of a hospital.

"Are you close to it?" he asked.

"Yeah, Dad. That's not far from me. Are you going too?"

"We are here now."

"Okay," said Telly, sighing and running a hand over his hair. "Okay, Dad. I'll be there real soon."

His father hung up.

—

Telly got into his car, having called out of work, canceled his lecture on surrealism, and combed his hair repeatedly until it became a mess worse than what he began with. He was beginning to think that his boss disliked him. It was practically the first time he had called out, thought Telly, and his boss was sort of a fucking bastard anyhow. His boss also had his hair slicked back all the time and he had one of those stupid Hitler 'staches. The bastard thought it looked great on him; Telly thought everyone had already shaved those stupid fuckers. But nevertheless, he was in his car driving to the hospital his father had told him to go to. He was listening to "I'll Be Seeing You" on the radio, trying to chant the words, but he did not know them.

On the way, he thought of Arnie. He was the true neighborhood man of his childhood. Arnie gave away his extra nickels, helped the little ones cross the streets. He refereed impromptu baseball games and had a firm handshake and his likeness to tomatoes bordered on concerning. He was a fond friend of Telly's parents. Arnie was the neighborhood man of Telly's youth, and Telly spun his story in his brain, collecting the little details he had on him: *his wife had the same birthday as him, he had the smallest sized feet on the block, he cut his hair extra short and ate sloppy—*

Arnie was now sixty-five years old in a hospital bed. He wouldn't turn sixty-sive. In 1919, he held Telly, a newborn, in his arms, when he came from the hospital to their wooden-planked, wobbly-floored, clear-windowed apartment in Boston.

In the early afternoon, Telly reached the hospital. Abiding by his own ways, he wandered down numerous hallways, until a nurse accosted him and demanded of where he needed to be. She seemed harried. He wondered why.

He was eventually led down a whitewashed hallway, past the strange, hushed hospital noises that often came from an injured mouth, and into a room where there were three partitions set up, separating each patient and the three beds, cutting the yellow walls in thirds. His mother and father stood next to the partition on the far right. As far as he could see, the other patients had no visitors. Telly turned to see the nurse had already left him. She had seemed to be in a hurry.

"Albertelli," said his father upon seeing his arrival. His navy button-up was neatly tucked into his trousers, his salt and pepper hair slicked back neatly, the wrinkles around his eyes from smiling tightly, chagrined, neat, blended smoothly into his scalp. He was an exact replica of his son.

"Oh, dear." His mother, Anita, rushed forward upon his arrival and grasped his forearm. Telly noticed the tears caught in her almond black eyes and thick eyelashes. Her brow had creased together, creating wrinkles that Telly was waiting to disappear. But they were permanent.

"Hi, Ma. Dad," Telly said politely. He had not seen them in three years.

"S'that Telly?" said a voice between his parents. They moved to the side and there was a very small hospital bed, one that would not fit Telly himself, and in it was Arnie.

"That guy on the other side here," said Arnie. "He's got his whole leg in a sling."

He did not look like the grinning, bumbling neighborhood man of Telly's youth. His old hair, which used to be coarse and coal-colored had lost its color, faded to a pale gray with the only remaining pieces clumped at his earlobes and temples, and his mouth was full of large teeth, large as they had always been, but discolored. The hollows under his eyes had sunken deeper into his corroding skin, the purple flesh spreading outward, and he had a blanket pulled tight up to his chin, which had loosened considerably and could not hold up his face for too long.

Oh, thought Telly, *Alright. He's actually dying.*

"Arnie!" hissed Anita, pressing a long finger to her lip. "He can hear."

"It's nothing he doesn't already know," murmured Arnie, a cynical smile present on his decaying mouth. "I'm glad you are not him, Telly."

"Hey, Arnie," said Telly, in the sort of tone he despised, that sympathizing, pitying tone. He had not seen the man in front of him since he was nineteen. "How are you?"

"Oh, you know. Dying. I've got heart problems," Arnie said as an explanation.

"Liver issues," corrected Telly's father. He saw that the usual stern expression had dulled down instead of softened.

"Well, it may as well be heart problems!" grunted Arnie. He made to roll over in his bed but cried out and chose to settle himself back into his first position.

"Oh, God," whispered Anita, clutching at her husband's sleeve.

"Don't worry yourself, dear. You know, Telly, you've gotten much older."

"Twenty-five," said his father.

"Twenty-six," said Telly. "I teach at a college nearby."

"He's a tutor," said his father.

"I lecture."

"Good God, shut up, will you?" said Arnie. "Get a wife. But don't go out shooting stuff."

"I wouldn't," said Telly.

"Yes, yes, yes," he murmured. "And the lakes become steam and then rain and they run off." He coughed.

"'Cause your wife would shoot you, you know. You go off shooting stuff, it's what you get." Arnie laughed at his words.

"I have what stuff they left behind," said Telly's father, and he held up a small duffle bag in his right hand, which Telly had not seen. He frowned and looked at Anita for an explanation. She just shook her head as if to say, *not now; I will tell you soon.*

"Good man, Claudio. Always a good man." Arnie sniffed. "How much is gone?"

"Most of it."

"And what did they find?"

"Nothing."

"Yeah, I thought that." Arnie laughed again, croaking. "They don't like us much now; they hated us much more a minute ago."

Telly was tempted to ask who "they" was.

"You have not gotten an apology yet," said his father. "But you will. I will get it for you."

"When I'm dead," sighed Arnie. "Don't hold your breath."

"I try not to."

Arnie coughed and his hand struggled to reach his stomach. "I'm going now. Best you go too. Good to see you, Telly. Teach well."

"We love you," Anita said in a rush, tears welling at the corners of her eyes.

"I will keep your things safe then," Telly's father said.

Arnie closed his eyes, but they could still hear his labored breathing.

"Ma," said Telly in a stage whisper. "What was he talking about? Who took his stuff?"

Anita smiled, her husband's arm on her shoulder. He spoke instead. "The government is targeting undocumented Italian immigrants, Albertelli. They raid houses."

"Looking for what? Why?"

"Italy is much more soft spoken now," he said. "We have come to America's side now. There is something to show for that." His voice told Telly not to ask further.

"Lord," coughed Arnie suddenly between them. He laughed slightly in his sleep.

"You still like to paint?" he mumbled.

-

Telly's parents were each eighteen years old when they arrived in America with their hats on their hearts and their watches set to Italian times. They touched the cold cobblestones with their palms and framed their faces for a photograph.

They met sometime during the middle of the first war at nineteen. Telly didn't know the details. The way they told it, they seemed to have known each other their whole lives.

They were married at twenty-one in a nice chapel. The guests sprinkled them with rice and they shared a glass of wine; real liquor, the kind that stained your mouth, and the kind they had not had in a very long time. When they kissed and when they pulled away, their teeth were maroon. Her dress was long and lovely. At night when they resolved their beliefs, they did so peace. They intertwined their thoughts, talking late into the night, until finding that the wine had spilt on the floor and stained the carpet. His mother once said that she could taste the liquor on her gums whenever she pleased. She said that was when she learned the sides to bitterness.

In 1919, they lived in a small apartment on Hanover Street. They made enough friends of well means to keep themselves comfortable. They had Telly, their only child, and made him a bed out of a small drawer. The air tasted thick and hot, like sweet milk and tobacco with a texture of mulch. His father went to work and came home regularly, until one day, he came home late. He walked in the door with a face of open endearment and a new folder in the bank. So they moved to a bigger house on the street, kept their friends comfortable with their own well means, and sent their child to school. Telly never took the time to understand his father's work. His father worked late, but he came home with restraint. He treated them gently, and some nights, if Telly could not sleep, he would leave his bedroom to find his parents sitting together. And they would not be touching, but he could sense the intertwining of their thoughts, and he could taste the red wine as if it was his own bottle.

They were never silly enough to take part in an American gamble. They watched themselves with sense, and gently, they revolved around their small world with care. And when Telly was old enough, they had one spectacular fight, and the gap between child and parents became an abyss. He drank wine repeatedly, often, regularly, until he no longer thought of his parents when he tasted the bitterness.

12.

In New Orleans, three women were typing together in a large, busy office space. There was a quick-fashioned way of going about business here. They placed the papers on the right desk and they wrote similar words and they signed it as Ulio the Adjutant General, for he could not write it himself.

"He's got the same name as my cousin," said one woman aloud.

"No kidding," said the second

"Yep. Same first name, last name."

"Sure it's not your cousin?"

"Yeah, my cousin's five. Lemme read it. The Secretary of War desires me to express... your son... Lieutenant James Fielder. Hah."

"Same spelling?" asked the third woman.

"Yeah."

"Guess there's a lotta James Fielders."

In the later years, I would meet the young James Fielder. He would curse my name when his day arrived, in exactly twenty years from this moment, and, finally, cry when I didn't speak. He did not know I was right next to him. I had my hands ready and the power of unconditional belief on my palms. I was trying to resuscitate him. It took years for me to realize that life doesn't work that way.

13.

It was decided at once that John and Jack Betchel would be the riflemen.

It was the obvious choice, thought Mckenzie as he picked his teeth at the mess hall tables. Their fingers moved fast enough, and they didn't hesitate the way Brenner did. And Brenner, thought Mckenzie, had to somehow have been the sneakiest of them all.

March had been full of exams. Many of them. His routine was flurried, rushed from building to building, and even then, he could hear the groups rolling in by the thousand every two hours. There were qualification cards (Mckenzie could not have listed much), military-issued clothing, barrack bags, chemical warfare, dismounted drills, marching and tactics, a thousand words that had no meaning before March, but in April, they made sense. They received their M1s, their packs and cartridge belts, canteens, mess kits, gas masks.

They would have thirty-six hours of physical training by the end of what? And they spent most of their time (124 hours) learning rifle marksmanship. Their first lesson in that gave John and Betchel a new talent.

5:55. Mckenzie never understood why they didn't just make it 6:00, or 5:50. The five-minute difference was miniscule. But ten minutes later, after he would resolve this conflict of getting up, and the platoons would be outside their barracks, lined up. They were counted off. They had fifteen minutes to get ready, in which they would make their bunks the special way they were taught so one could bounce a dime off of them, put their uniforms on, gather equipment, and watch the older members shave, since they were young enough to not grow shit. The group headed outside for "morning formation." Mckenzie had never heard of that before his arrival, but he knew a thing or two about it now. So they assembled on the drill field, and after days of practice and Stroshine getting his ass handed to him (the squad watched happily; they disliked him after the first conversation), they were able to assemble with competence.

Oftentimes, Mckenzie would see Sergeant Travers's eyes glaze over, and he would wonder if he ever saw such strange eyes before. Mckenzie had never met such a strange man. He was different from the other Sergeants. He didn't have to try to have a hold over his troops.

They ate breakfast at 6:20, in thirty minutes, in the mess hall, which could hold over 150 men. Mckenzie stood in line with his Bakelite tray and spoke with John and Lee, John who was always alert and awake, and Lee who hated mornings. The squad primarily sat close together, Lee next to John, and Mckenzie across from them. They found an enjoyable presence in Vicky Halsted and William White, the latter of whom was funny enough to entertain them for the entire meal. They ate pork and bacon and canned vegetables, and timed how many seconds it took for John to drink his entire glass of milk, which he swore he dreamt of in eager excitement at night. Lee took two minutes off his breakfast time to sit at the table in silence, balancing his head between his hands and staring down at the table. He was praying, John told Mckenzie in a whisper.

Lee did this every morning at the same time for the rest of his life. For exactly sixty-two years after I first witnessed his prayers, I had an appointment every morning at 6:50, where I listened to Lee Collins' thoughts. Not once did they disappoint.

They, along with the rest of the men, briefly returned to the barracks. 7:00 to 7:15. They gathered their gear and strapped their gear to themselves with the given equipment, glued themselves together in the necessary way to succeed. They assembled on their company street, a place I never visited, and marched for forty-five minutes, in perfect formation, Lee looking grimly on, John and Mckenzie grinning and keeping their laughter inside, toward the Exercise Field. I tried my best not to go there, either.

"Saving fuel," said Travers one day on their march after belittling Mike Stroshine, who quickly became the group's scapegoat.

"Saving fuel," Mckenzie repeated later to John. "S'why we can't get rides on trucks and whatnot."

Eight a.m. to 5:30 was training. Classrooms after classroom. Mckenzie's fingers ached after days of retracting his rifle one thousand times, while he lay on his stomach, reloading and unloading, watching Lee fiddle with a bullet between his ring finger and thumb, running down dirt lanes with Forrest Burns, the arrogantly fast ass, and sprinting ahead, until John subtly nosed dust at his head with the toe of his boot.

Dinner took place at midday. It was essentially lunch.

Their exercises, in which Mckenzie was somehow average and John excelled, contributed to their busyness. They did marching and running drills with long, heavy matched guns, and took on obstacle courses with Sammy's snide remarks in their ears; these words especially made John laugh. They did pushups, sit ups, jumping jacks with Jack Betchel beating them all into the sand, his wedding band gleaming sun into their eyes. Mass exercise and contests, breaks in the afternoon, broken Army-issued boots, hot sun, and sore knuckles: these were the burdens of Mckenzie's days and he learned to love them so.

They clambered over fences and lowered themselves quickly into five-foot trenches, weaved through pickets, ditches, and ropes, with twenty-foot catwalks. They had lucid dreams at night where they kicked their feet out in dramatic, effective poses. Sometimes Mckenzie woke in the middle of the night in a curious cold sweat hearing live ammunition like he would in the daytime, crawling in mud. It never bothered him until it was time to sleep.

Classes started. Mckenzie and most of the other men never enjoyed these as much as Lee did. He enjoyed sitting in the cooler air, listening to someone ramble about war indoctrination, sexual education, and military courtesy. Lee was a born gentleman. Lectures became movies, and lecturers became recently released officers from North Africa, Leningrad, and New Guinea battlefields, the latter's paleness darkening from the returning warmth of spring in the states.

One hundred twenty-six hours were devoted lovingly to rifle marksmanship because, as Mckenzie saw the minute of his arrival, guns were loved. Many in the group, like John, Jack Betchel, and Al

Halsted enjoyed the mysterious nature of weapons. Vicky Halsted and Joe Marshall were unfortunately untalented as such, Kenneth Greene becoming a king, and the rest were average. The M1 rifle became a great deal of happiness and dread for the troop. So, so many positions, Mckenzie began to sleep with his fingers in the correct placement. Loop sling, prone position, kneeling position, trigger squeezing, loading fresh clips, and numerous exercises that involved his chin pressed to his chest and his hands blindly moving. They learned field stripping and how to conduct proper maintenance, and a million movements Travers made on the first afternoon now had names. Oftentimes, Sid Dorman and William White could be found conversing about the qualification that would take place in the last month of basic training. They shot at moving silhouettes and cleaned bathroom toilets, Lee covering his grin under his brush as he knelt on cold tiles and swept at the facial hair dusting the ground.

There were more than one type of grenade apparently, and John would gleefully fake throws at Marshall, who would shriek and dive to the ground. Travers said that his execution was good enough, but to cut the screaming, lest he wanted to spot Fritz up close. Standing or kneeling positions were taught their roles, and suddenly Mckenzie would be standing with a grenade in his right hand, his powerful hand. The others would be crouched in the makeshift grenade pit, throwing far fewer explosive bits at each other, and then bayonets, which Sammy Brenner had an intense hatred for. Travers suggested that Brenner simply did not understand the physics behind parry and thrust, and instead of sulking, Brenner just chuckled, a strange occurrence for him, and punched the straw-filled bags with his iron fist.

Then there were the days when Mckenzie would whirl around and Lee stood before him with a gas mask closed around his brown sullen eyes and shaking his head at White's antics. They watched White waving his hands above his head, while thirteen men hovered around the "gas chamber," a name that commenced commentary from John for weeks. Mckenzie most enjoyed their land navigation practice in the forests, where they concealed themselves behind bushes with ease and tinkered with compasses. By 6:45 p.m., they dropped off their field equipment, and went to the mess hall for supper.

Training went on like this for a month. The men in the squad had their roles, and I had mine. Jack Betchel and John were quick with a trigger, Joe whistled bob-white better than anyone, Sammy Brenner and Al Halsted could stomp on you within a second of your mistake, Sid Dorman and Forrest Burns were the fastest of the fast, William White could make a somber fellow break into laughter at a funeral, Mike Stroshine and Vicky Halsted were slight assholes and tentatively talented with a grenade below the wrist, Lee and Mckenzie completed navigation with flying colors, and Kenneth Rupert Greene jumped awake every night at two o'clock. He cried lonesomely, and went back under the covers. By the end of the war, there were circles under his eyes as dark as the fresh dirt from his grave.

14.

Briefly, I digress from our story. I'll tell you something about me. I guess I'd like to be a reliable narrator.

Once someone had asked me about sin. He was a newcomer, years past this story, delivered to me by fairytale friends of mine, and he was far too young. He knew me well and I found I did not know him at all. He had read my stories, the ones before my lonesome years, and he asked me, spirit to spirited, about sin. He had been taught certain ways to go about living, and the way people had been behaving was destroying a way of life that he immersed himself in. There was such a thing as repercussions, he told me. He taught me about karma, that prehistoric idea I never knew had a meaning. It's an idea that is brought into church under another name, one that mystical women with shawls draped around their shoulders would tell you about with your palm open to their eyes. There would be consequences, he said, and I would bring them on.

Would I? I said. I knew nothing of the sort. No one had informed me of my own job before. I was bewildered.

That is what they have told me, in writing, he said. *You are ever present and forgiving. You love me.*

I could have loved him. His words were thoughtful.

Writing is not real, even when it comes from the truth, I said to him. *It is not real. All fantasy.*

Even when it's about real life? he asked me.

Yes. The fighting isn't real. So close your eyes. And he did. I smiled, although he could not see it, and told him that I knew nothing of sin, I knew nothing of writing. The first part had been a lie. I had seen sin since the beginning of my creation, since the days when I believed I was made to halt all selfish decisions, more sin than I had ever believed capable of the world. I lied and hoped my lying abilities were made to be extremely good in that story he had told me about. But the second part was true. I knew nothing of writing, nothing of what the people believed were the facts about me. I had never opened a book and chosen to learn about humans; I had never liked writers. But the boy was my introduction. He spun pretty tales, things that had never happened and will never happen in the course of history, and he told me legends and made the past a miracle. His words were thoughtful and they would never progress into anything better. For a moment, as I sat here writing this to you, I thought that maybe the boy was my creator, that he had written all those stories about me that people believed to be fact, and that he had come to me, with open arms, to discover if it was real. But I put the notion away. He was just too young.

15.

If you happened to be on the highway and took a random exit, say Exit 6, in the evening in the summer of 1935, you would see one of the best sunsets of your life. But it was not 1935 anymore, although Telly still had nothing to do. He turned his car through Exit 6 anyhow, at 6:30 p.m., and did not notice the red tops of the sun sinking below the pine trees, the orange streaks through the sky that blended into the blue. His hands gripped the steering wheel tightly; his radio played "I'll Be Seeing You."

Exit 6 was chosen at random for Telly, but it happened to be one that led straight to a little town off the between tracks. When one spoke of the East Coast, this town was rarely not cast aside. Telly had never heard of it. In fact, he drove past the welcome sign without any concern or notice, his rickety Ford creaking heavily over the bumps in the road and narrowly missing a pothole, so narrowly that only an otherworldly being could have stopped it. He thought of Arnie, dying in a hospital alone. Here he had taken this strange drive to forget about the man, and he was still thinking about it. He had been thinking, alone in his house, that he had never really seen death before, and this was a fact he was strangely ashamed of. So he got into his car and drove to where the voices of people could drown out his thoughts. The radio hissed; the music notes spun in the air, and Telly turned his vehicle down a busier pathway at the very last second, and he found himself in front of a diner.

It was a twenty-four-hour diner, minutes off of the highway with servers who were less than fortunate in their pay. The glowing light sign flickered and the windows were warm and had crickets chirping below them. In the back of the building two young children played together under the picnic tables, rolling in the April grass. Slats of shadows and neon red lights were decorated in stripes on the pavement. The strange spring heat of the night reflected off the parked black cars of the employers—which had been sitting there for hours—and Telly forced the picturesque scene into his memory for later, an image to possibly be used in a drawing of sorts. Dimly, one could hear the talkative waitresses giggling behind the empty counters, the sloshing, messy pour of hot coffee with an unsteady hand, and the heavy footsteps belonging to a working man in loafers as he tapped his feet and watched his wife across the booth from him finish her champagne. The two children outside were still laughing, covered in an abnormal amount of grass stains that, Telly imagined, would send their mother into a fit of rage when she spotted them. He pictured them arriving home with their mother, who upon opening the door, saw her husband and launched into a routine telling off when he laughed at his children's antics. It smelled of cinnamon butter and long days.

Telly was enjoying this scenario in his parked vehicle when the door to the diner swung open gently, like a breeze had carried it, and he saw the women who had exited. There were three women, all wearing red shirts which matched the regular design of the diner. One, the oldest, was round and short. The woman who seemed Telly's age had her brown hair tucked into the collar behind her neck. The very youngest, who could not have been older than seventeen, was as freckled as a youngster could be. The three women laughed, shaking their heads over some scene they had all witnessed. The oldest and youngest began walking off toward their car on the other side of the parking lot, leaving the brown-haired girl still chuckling and waving goodbye outside the front of the diner. She looked *interesting*. Somehow, she presented herself as a distraction.

Telly got out of his car before he could stop himself and found himself standing directly in front of the brown-haired woman so fast he barely noticed. She blinked several times at his sudden appearance.

"Sorry, am I in your way?" said the woman, looking back at the entrance to the diner. Her voice was a dry kind of rumble, but not unpleasant.

"No, not at all." Telly flapped his hands against his stomach leisurely. "Please, stand there as long as you'd like."

"Ok," she confusedly agreed with him. "Can I help you with something?"

"Are you still working?"

"The diner is still open. We're all hours."

"Are *you* still working then?"

"No. Can I ask what this is about?"

"No." Telly immediately strode to the passenger side of his car, opened the door, and looked at the waitress expectedly. Her face creased into more layers of confusion. Her limbs were abnormally skinny so that her uniform hung off her, she was extraordinarily tall, an inch or two below Telly, and her hair and eyes were almost exactly the average shade of brown. Her mouth was long on the sides, and her nose had no curves at all and the slope was straight. She was sort of *strange*, now that he thought of it. But he supposed that he fit right in with that title.

"Yes, you can ask what this is about." Telly sighed, as she did not seem to understand at all. Although, he knew he was being slightly fucking insane.

"Are you trying to kill me?" she said. She was acting out "bored," possibly to defend herself, and Telly felt guilty about it. She *was* sort of intriguing in the way that she didn't seem to care much about his presence.

"What? No. Jesus." Telly frowned.

"Then what is this about?"

"I want to take you out."

"You were really unclear about it. I don't get taken out much." The woman shifted so all her weight leaned on her right side and took a lighter and cigarette from her purse. "Can I smoke?"

"You're asking me permission?"

"Some people don't like the smoke. It hurts your eyes sometimes." She seemed somehow much more comfortable now that she had seen his reaction to the question on if she was going to be an attempted murder project.

"I'm alright with it." He carefully watched her light it, noticing how her fingers held the lighter between her ring and pointer, and how her thumb twisted it into a flame.

"Where would you like to take me?"

"Where would you like to go?"

"Why not right here?" She gestured to the diner with her cigarette. "It's nice. We are all hours."

"You just got done working here."

"Haven't you just finished eating here?"

"No, why would you believe that?"

"Because you were sitting in your car outside the diner. I thought you had just finished your meal."

"No. I just arrived about a minute ago. I don't believe I've ever been here before."

"Well it's nice. We're all hours."

"You just mentioned that lovely plus."

She sighed. "Alright. Shall we go in?"

"After you."

The diner bells rang as she pushed open the door. Her coworker at the front table looked up nonchalantly and, spotting the woman, said loudly, "You forget something?"

"No. I'm on a date, I guess."

The waitress paused her wiping down the table and looked at Telly, who stood slightly behind his new friend. He nodded as politely as one could.

"Oh. Good to see you. It's nice here. We're all hours," said the waitress uninterestedly before resuming her tasks.

"He's a lover of diners," Telly's date announced. "He likes to sit in parking lots of these types and tempt himself with the smell of milkshakes."

"Personally, I'd torture myself with the Coney Island," said the waitress.

"I'm Telly."

"That's neat. Here's your table, to my troubles."

The two of them sat down on opposite sides and the woman turned her attention to the menu, which Telly recognized she probably needn't look at. She'd read it a million times.

"I'm Telly," he said again.

"That's an odd sort of name, don't you think?" she said, looking down at the menu. "Is that rude to say? Are you offended by that?"

"I'm never offended."

"So you're mellow."

"Sure."

"Telly, what's an average day for yourself? I'm finding it hard to believe you would take it upon yourself to sit in diner parking lots in hopes of finding a woman every night. If that's your actual thing, then you're a strange guy, forgive me if that's rude. Maybe it's fate."

"Fate?"

"Yes, Telly." She grinned with the teeth on the sides of her mouth peeking out. "You don't nearly do this as much as I presumed. So on the day you happen to a diner and sit in the parking lot, you find me and ask me to dinner. What are the chances of this happening again to you, and the woman saying yes?"

Telly thought about this for a moment. "Should I feel insulted by that?"

"God, no."

"Alright," he said. "Alright, good. What is your name?"

"Telly, promise this is not your attempt on my life."

"I'm not leaning toward murdering you."

"Alright, good. Then I'm June."

"As in the month?"

"Yes."

"That makes a lot of sense to me," said Telly. "You're very 'summer' acting. You have the physique of someone who liked to swim as a child."

"I didn't really like to swim. And I was born in January. But I am guessing that's a compliment."

"Oh, yeah. It was intended as one."

"May I ask some questions? Get-to-know-you questions, if you will?"

"I didn't expect an interrogation, but as I have nothing else to do, fire away," said Telly, finding himself smiling dryly. He was liking this. He liked that every bit of June was bright and lucid, like a painting from only reds and blues.

His dinner partner wore a shit-eating grin that leered at him like a cat. "Alright," June announced. "I've got one. Where are you from?"

"I was born in Boston. Now you."

"Somewhere along the coast. I was born right out on the streets, you know."

"Really? You don't say."

"Yes. I was several weeks early. I suppose they have a name for that sort of birth—"

"Premature."

"Yes, yes. And my mother rushed out of the house, raced to my father's laundromat, and told him I was coming. She had no idea how to get to the hospital. So, of course, they got into the car, but they didn't end up too far. I was born in January, you know."

"I guessed as much, June. How come your mother did not know her way to the hospital?" asked Telly, leaning forward on his elbows.

"I don't rightfully know."

"That's very irresponsible of your parents, if you don't mind me telling you so," he said. "What if you had been born at home and came out with three heads?"

"I suspect I wouldn't be sitting here if that had happened."

"I'm asking the question now?"

"Yes."

"Did you go to school? If so, where?"

June nodded rapidly, then contradictorily said, "No, no. I don't think I'm smart enough. It does not interest me much."

"You're probably plenty smart enough."

"I think it doesn't quite matter if that's true or not. College isn't for me. How about you?"

"I attended an arts school. My mother happened to be an acquaintance of a professor there."

"Did you really? Are you agreeable in much of that?"

"Much of what?"

June shrugged. Her brown children's bangs dipped into her brows. "The arts."

"I'm alright, I think."

"Can I see some of it?"

"Some of what?"

"Your work. Like, your art."

"No. Well, I'm not done with it yet."

"Nothing? You've finished nothing then?"

"Jesus, I guess when you put it like that." He didn't mean for the bite to be present in his voice but it was.

The pair ordered two milkshakes in cold glasses that dripped condensation and liquid sugar down the sides, sucked at them with the straws hanging from the corners of their mouths, and tapped their feet rhythmically on the tiled floor. Behind the kitchen counters, the workers were packing up and folding away their aprons.

They danced. They drank their drinks dry and pushed them toward the edge of the counter. June fiddled a quarter and she stuck it in the jukebox behind their booth. Small cutouts of Dick Tracy's face and the Andrews Sisters were glued to the machine in a way so they popped out unexpectedly. They listened to "In The Blue Light" and spun slowly around the diner, their sneakers squeaking against the newly polished floors, Telly's face bent down to look at June, whose face was bent up to look at him, her bangs hung over her eyebrows again, a small crease between them. She was thinking very hard, singing the words in her head. I watched them, the typical lovers of the decade, their hands brushing at the other's arms, their noses pointed toward the other's ears.

They wandered outside, leaving cash on the table, and bumped into cars, laughing. I looked at them from the diner window, attempting to be as quiet as possible. "Moonlight Serenade" was still ringing out on the jukebox and I thought of Mckenzie subconsciously. Telly and June were still laughing away into the night, a sound still audible behind the rumble of car engines. They were already well on their way, and had no idea of it.

16.

There came a day when Joe Marshall could not get out of bed, even as they were lining up, packing their gear, standing outside for attendance, and marching to the field. Not even as they were finishing with breakfast (cut short for their group), John shoving an orange down Lee's pants for later, and trekking back to their barracks, Travers at the head of them. He opened the doors to the barrack.

"Marshall!" called Travers. He stood stock still in the doorway and then walked quickly inside. He made a ruckus, and the others followed quickly behind him.

"Sir," said John. "Ah, Cap."

"What is it, St. Dennis?"

"Cap, he's got a plague," said John vaguely.

It certainly appeared to Mckenzie that Joe did. He was ghastly, deathly, immobile, pale, unimaginably still in his bed, the covers pulled up to his chin as if his mother had tucked him in. He was asleep. I watched the previous night as Lee shushed Marshall's complaints of 'not being right headed' and tucked him into the mattress. I knew what would be coming.

"It's seven o'clock," said Al Halsted. "He oughta be up now. We's got to get a'moving."

"Shut up, Halsted," said Mckenzie.

"It's the goddamn schedule, *Rye.*"

"Well, shuck the damn schedule, Al," Mike Stroshine edged in. "He's sick, can't you see?"

"Marshall." Travers looked over Joe's form in his bed, not moving an inch.

"He's dead," said Forrest Burns dully. "He's dead. We got here too late."

"Hey, won't you shut the fuck up then? You're not coming to the effing wake."

"S'not gonna be a wake when he's looking like that."

"Keep up your talking," Lee said, looking each guy in the eye. "I swear I'll hit you right in your mouth." It was the first threat Mckenzie had heard from Lee's mouth and it simultaneously amused and terrified him. Either way, they did not keep up their talking.

"I think you'd be doing Forrest a favor with that, Collins. Look at his fucking chompers. I gave him a piece of bread at breakfast the other day, and he almost bit my fucking hand off," said Sammy Brenner.

Al Halsted quite genuinely laughed out loud, as though the joke was written for him, and although it was painfully unfunny.

"Cap," questioned John. He was tilting back and forth on his toes at the front of the group. "Cap, what's the diagnosis?"

And it sounds selfish, but Mckenzie didn't realize until that moment that Marshall and Lee and John, they had grown up together, joined together, and it would be natural for them to care for each other, although Lee and John often showed disdain for Joe.

Travers stared down at Marshall for another minute. Then he stepped back and faced the men. "Heat fever," he said. "Alright. That's that. Halsted—Vicky Halsted, go get a doctor. Run off now." Vicky did so.

"Cap?" said Jack Betchel. "Heat fever?"

"Heat fever?" John frowned incredulously.

"Fuck is that?" said Will White, who had once lived at the very highest point of northern Maine.

"Heat's got to him, that's all?" said Al.

"Why don't you say that again while *you're* laying there all dead in *your* bed—"

"I swear to God, I swear, you better shut your goddamn—"

"He's not dead," said Mckenzie. "He's breathing."

"Okay, well, it was a fucking joke, Rye."

"Shut up," murmured Kenneth Green. Nobody noticed him.

"It was a dumb joke anyway, White," Betchel said.

"You know, I'm gonna fuck your wife one a' these days—"

"Shut up, shut up!" shouted John, waving his hands over his head, turning to glare at the group. "Shut up. I want a bullet in my head 'cause of you lot."

"Aww, don't say that, John."

"Yeah, that's a bit insensitive."

"Hey," said Green. When nobody looked his way, he said louder, "Hey! How'd John's screaming not wake up Marshall?"

Travers stared for a moment, then turned back to Marshall.

"He's got the plague, you said?" said Travers.

"No, Cap. I was joking, I mean. I haven't got a clue what's the matter."

"Alright. Well. Get on with your day, fellas."

"Sir, I think *I* should *walk him* down to the infirmary," said John. His arms were crossed. He was the kind of man whose thoughts you could see run out of his ears.

"You have to shake him up first," said Travers and he stepped aside. John hesitantly walked closer to Marshall's sleeping, lifeless form in bed and looked down at him for a moment. And gently, John tapped his shoulder very fast.

"Joe?" he said. "C'mon, we have to get you up."

Joe Marshall's carrot top hair was brushed back, exposing his forehead. It was eerily pale with bits of dotted fluid painting the small hairs near his scalp. He had a nauseating spell about him, as though he had been entranced, and his nose was pink, as though he had been marching through Russian borders without his government-issued boots. Joe knew a man who had made that walk. He said he would not do it again.

In the end John waited for Vicky Halsted to bring back the doctor. Travers watched over the doctor who watched over Joe, and told the group to get on with it. But John did not move, so the others did not move. It was a regular occurrence, John doing something and the others doing the same. However, by lunch, the men decided that they were hungry. They left for the mess hall, leaving John watching Travers and Travers watching the doctor and the doctor watching Joe and Joe watching me. He was dreaming about me. It was the first dream he'd had in a while.

John made an appearance at dinner. He found Mckenzie and Lee eating pork and rolls while they listened to Vicky and White debate over how much cash they obtained in their youths.

"I'll call you Two-Wallet-White," said Vicky. "You think the Army will ever find out you're a picker?"

"Hi, John," said Lee to John, who was sitting down beside him. He didn't speak for a moment; he just reached for a roll, tore it into three pieces, and began to eat.

"John, how's Marshall?" White asked.

"He's alright, I guess," said John very matter-of-factly, his mouth still full. "He's got some sort of a cold in the head, but he'll be okay soon enough."

"That's good, John," said Lee.

"Micky?"

It was a nickname meant for Mckenzie, something only John dared to call him. Mckenzie turned to look at his big-eared, playful friend. He was looking back. Slightly upset-looking, might I add.

"What're you doing here anyhow, Micky?" said John, grinning with an unhappy expression. "You're not like Lee 'n' Joe. Or Will here. You didn't have to be here, like, you really didn't. What're you doing here?"

"He's here for America," said Vicky with a mouthful of meat. They ignored him.

Mckenzie only said, "Are you upset with me? 'Cause I don't have to be here? Genuinely?"

John looked surprised, all tenseness washing away from his face. "Course not."

"Ok. Because you don't really have a right to be." John's eyes creased and wrinkled at the corner.

"I'm not upset with you. But, I don't know. I don't know if I really wanna be here anymore."

It all felt very familiar to me. Something I had witnessed long ago, maybe.

17.

In 1941, I was stationed in a very cold French place with hundreds of boys who were stationed there too. The refuge was hardly safe. The boys were given heavy green blankets and mugs of hot coffee that tasted of mushed up soil. They sat on the hard ground against the poles of hoisted tents and passed around photographs and cigarettes. A French man had given a group of them a pack; he lit their cigarettes for them and talked, but they could not understand what he was saying, nor if they were going to die or what position he held. The ground had no snow.

I tried to listen to their stories. Understand their ways. Their stories were all different from mine, I who have no limit on living, no limit on witnessing, no dotted line saying "sign here," "sign for immortality." I spoke only the language of the people, or I tried to. But I didn't understand their way. They said lots of words I could not inquire the meanings of. I was curious because I thought that I had invented foreign words.

One boy caught my eye. Everyone crowded around him the most, but he talked little. He was looking at a photograph of his mother that he kept on the inside of his shirt, next to his heart. She was a nice woman. She had one of those faces and you could just tell it.

"Tell me your theory again," said a boy beside the one holding the picture.

"You've heard it before," he said.

"Tell it again. You sound so smart when you are telling me things."

He was talking about a chess game. Somebody called Fritz, except he was a collection of people, yet only one man. He spoke of an endgame and pawns on the board. He said the pieces were moving and that they were the pieces and that the pieces were dying on white squares instead of black. He said that there was something very wrong with dying in the snow. The red stained it all over until it was no longer a very Merry Christmas, Hallelujah. He told the others that there was something to be said about the pawns. He said that it was a wonder that the pawns had not turned to their commanding hands and wondered why, and it was. He noticed that everyone was armed nowadays and nobody took the winning shot. He asked around the group, he asked them why. They did not give him an answer, so he continued. He said there could be no winning shot if the leaders were not facing guns. He asked them if Churchill had children.

By morning, it was snowing white. By evening it was red.

May.

3

What ends a war?

Liberation had arrived in Europe. Telly did not know the meaning of this word, or what it would mean for himself, but he knew what it would bring. As for me, I sat patiently in front of a mirror for the last days of April. I raised my hand in a mock salute.

The Soviets were closing the gap toward Berlin in the days leading up to liberation. One and one met at the River Elbe, and an army was halved. I heard that they were married in a bunker under the Reich Chancellery headquarters. They were both dead a day later.

Carrie and Rico sat in front of their radio on the first day of May. The baby was down for a nap. Frank and Donna played with the curtains.

For a few days it was mostly confusing to the entire world. It was not, as German officials said, a death fighting in combat, fighting Bolshevism. It was not a disease-ridden lay overseas, and he did not die the year before. Only I understood the details of what had happened; I saw it right before my eyes, and I think he saw me too, before he loaded the gun or took the capsule, or even before he was burnt to the remains of his teeth. He is one of the few memories I have wanted to lose.

So the old story goes, I guess, Hitler and his girl killed themselves in a combination of ways in their Berlin bunker, a place soon to be rubble below my feet. They were married for perhaps thirty-six hours. I had never known such extreme forms of escaping the one who you gave a ring. He wrote his successor to be Grand Admiral Karl Doenitz, and he took his poison and his bullet with pride. He looked me in the eye as he did it.

Why'd you do this? I asked him, because I do not know everything.

He did not answer. He didn't appear to hear me, although he was very close already; I could tell he was slipping. But his eyes were still on mine. When I turned around, I realized he was focused on a burning candle balanced behind me on his desk. He had seen right through me. I could have blown out the candle and danced in its smoke. It wouldn't have mattered. He wouldn't have seen me.

When I saw his wife, she was going that very second. She didn't see me either.

God-fearing, I said.

Love knows no bounds. Especially if it isn't love.

—

"Who's home?" called Telly into the entrance hallway. Evidently, Frank was, as he came tearing into the room.

"Hi, buddy," said Telly and Frank shook his hand, just as he taught him.

What ends a war?

Maybe a handshake. Something that simple.

"Come quick now!" yelled Rico from the other room. "Some man's down."

"Who's that now?"

He found them in the living room, sitting tangled together on the sofa in front of the radio, which balanced precariously on a footstool.

"You see," said Carrie before turning to look him straight in the eye. She seemed giddy with joy. "They got him now. They knew it was coming."

"He killed himself," Rico added.

"Who did?"

"The Fuhrer himself, of course. My mother," she said, "is ecstatic. She called me this morning with the news. I put the radio on, called you..."

"The fuck is that?" said Telly, sitting down in the armchair across from the parents. He brought his legs up as Frank and Donna rushed by, giggling.

"The Fuhrer?"

"Yeah."

"Hitler."

"Oh." Telly had heard of him. "Oh. Holy shit."

"Quit swearing, I got kids with ears, Tel," said Rico.

"Aw, they aren't listening."

"Holy shit!" shouted Frank, and Donna giggled louder, her blonde curls drooping over her small, cherub face.

"You just—" Rico sighed, running his hands over his eyes and groaning. "This isn't really fit for the kids to be hearing." He motioned to the radio. It was saying something about Europe, of course.

"I should—"

"No, I got them. C'mere. Come with Dad." Rico's two oldest children followed him into the hallway. "Can you guys play here, for just a moment?"

"The baby, Rico! Shh." Carrie smiled at Telly and put a finger to her lips.

"So he killed himself? Truly?" asked Telly.

Carrie turned to him. "Mhm. The sad part about it was, well, I bet he only did it because they were closing in on him. Germany couldn't have won."

"Really?"

"Yes. You know…" She sighed grimly and shook her head, those shimmering blue eyes narrowed. "His girlfriend killed herself too."

"No kidding. Are you serious?"

"Mhm. Together. Well, I should say wife. They were married, I think. And to think, they didn't die because they thought they were guilty."

"Someone will now," Telly said matter-of-factly. "Now that he's up there. He'll suffer eternal damnation, so they say."

"I suppose," said Carrie. "I wish it could happen right here. On Earth, I mean. I'd like to see that. I can think of many people who'd like to see that."

"You aren't glad he's all dead then?"

"I'm okay with his death, of course, of course I am. But I wish it was not at his own hands. You know, maybe he'd feel the way all those innocents did. He deserved a punishment in front of all those people. I think he took the easy way out."

"Is death an easy possibility, you think?"

"I think so."

"You know," said Telly. "I told Mckenzie. Before he left. I told him to just shoot and shoot and to not look at those folks he's getting. I don't even know if that *is* how it works. I guess it is."

"That's the only way he'll stay alive," Carrie delivered gently.

"Yes, but he doesn't have to think how I do. I'll turn him into some psycho. God, he really doesn't have to think how I do. I'd rather him not turn into some bloody-handed brute. Not that *I* am. But you—yeah. And I told him not to be dumb. I told him, *don't be fucking stupid*. But he's got more sense than I do, so of course he'll end up being fucking stupid at some point."

"You give some strange advice," said Carrie.

It was quiet for a moment. Then Telly said very quietly, like a child, "What did Hitler do?"

She smiled in a tight way. Sort of stiff and sad. "I read about what he did, probably a tiny fraction of what he orchestrated, but it was enough for me."

"He was a bad man, then. And if anyone deserved death it would be him."

"Sometimes I think maybe only the good deserve death," she said.

"'Cause the world's so screwed up, that's why. We fight all the time over pebble-sized shit. No good man belongs here."

"That's one way of seeing it," said Carrie. "How's your girl?"

"Girl, what girl?" demanded Rico as he returned from his children's antics, a wiggling grin on his face. He sat down next to his wife and tapped his feet rhythmically.

Carrie switched the radio off. "Telly's got a girlfriend." She turned to Telly. "Don't you?"

"No way in hell."

"I call on her sometimes. We go out to eat. We take many walks and talk a lot on the telephone at night," said Telly simply, shrugging. "I think she's encouraged by me so far."

"Yeah well, you're just a catch. What's her name?"

"June," he said and bit the inside corner of his mouth to stop from showing all his teeth. "We met at a diner. Or, a diner parking lot."

"A parking lot? That is romantic."

"You've no romantic bone in your body, funny boy."

"Is she in love with how much of a tragic artist you are?"

"You know, she is."

"I wanna meet her and impress her with all sorts of business stats." Rico waved his hands as though shooting a basketball. "Here, today on Wall Street, drum roll please for the numbers! Was she born in June?"

"No, she was born in January. I asked. On the side of the road as well."

"No. Was she?"

"Yeah."

"That means she is going to have your children on the side of a road."

"In some dark alley."

"Yeah. And your baby will come out with angry biceps and a twisted dick."

"That was you as a baby. You're getting all mixed up."

"Actually," Rico frowned and considered. "I haven't got a clue what goes on in Wall Street."

"Neither do I. Carrie?"

Carrie had been looking out the window with a lonely expression on her face, and Telly suddenly feared that she was really, *really* thinking about the draft law. What it meant. Why it was there. But then her eyes crinkled with thoughtfulness. "If you're asking all these questions now, you should be wondering why it is possible for numbers to change a person's life."

"The number of nipples Telly's baby will be born with will change his life."

"That baby will have fewer nipples than you did, no matter the number," she said.

19.

The boys arrived in the mess hall one morning and questioned Travers about John's absence.

Travers brushed it off. He said that John was off doing one of his punishments somewhere on the base, scouring the floors of a bathroom maybe. He had a slightly smart mouth, and it was funny unless he was overheard by someone with a higher rank than him.

The mess hall breakfast line was filling fast. Lee and Mckenzie swiftly cut in front of two men who were not paying attention, and began to scout for John. They spotted him scrubbing at a display case at the far end of the hall. It was the only sign of vanity over the entire expanse of the camp, and Mckenzie found himself looking at it often while he ate. It wasn't an item that needed cleaning; I understood John's only purpose was to look like the help, but he cleaned with such vigor, and with a big grin on his face, and this led me to believe he was nowhere near ashamed.

He had a radio near him. One of those radios that were in abundance in war, the ones that played lighthearted music and made lousy jokes.

John flipped the dial. The music got louder.

Mckenzie nudged Lee.

"You almost made me drop my tray, Rye."

"Look at John," he said.

Their common table members were looking at John crouching on the ground and fiddling with the radio. From across the room, they could hear a soft hum of the music. Men closer to him were staring. Some were smiling.

"They're gonna eat him up for this," said White.

They stood up, leaving their trays on the table, and cautiously walked closer to where a small group was forming around the radio. It was playing "Cheek to Cheek" and John was dancing.

Mckenzie laughed out loud. John was spinning ridiculously in his fucking Army uniform and all, doing strange twists and waving his arms about, singing the words to this stupid song that all the men knew by heart. The men were clapping, too. It was painfully corny and Mckenzie almost wished he'd stop. John made a spectacular turn and pointed at Lee, singing words that Mckenzie could no longer hear over the men laughing at him, nor over the incoming steps of superiors. Lee shook his head, squeezed his lips out of a smile, and rolled his eyes. He was clever, sharp, and inherently wicked below the very basic brain powers, and his friend was John, the John who christened the mess hall, the John who drank glass after glass of whole milk, the John who knew the words to bad songs. He liked to sing, too. John liked just about everything in those days.

He had to clean the bathrooms for a week.

After the old hell man was gone, as Brenner called him, the few days after were disorganized. The German front was receding into the ground, and the Allies hadn't needed to pull the trigger yet. Naturally, the boys spent a Sunday night at an officer's bar close by; they had nudged their ways in, the whole group of them, excluding Travers, and added on a Colonel or something, a middle-aged man who called himself their watchman and whose name Mckenzie forgot immediately.

Mckenzie sat at a table with Lee and Jack Betchel, both who swore they did not like to drink. He was quiet. He was reading over a letter to send to his parents. He didn't bother writing out important locations and information, as it would get redacted anyhow. Lee and Jack were playing a card game and drinking Cokes.

White and Stroshine were making it a contest to see who could dance with the most girls after taking three shots in a row. White wobbled back and forth, bumping into their table, his bony hands clutching weakly at a heart-faced girl's waist, who was giggling at his drunken demeanor and whose name Mckenzie caught to possibly be Lily. Stroshine watched sullenly from the side.

Marshall, having recovered from his bout of illness, was talking at the bar with John, Vicky, and Brenner. They yelled at each other over the talking of other military officers with the same idea as them, their faces obscenely red. John was waving his beer above his head, and it was continuously slopping onto the counter. Al and Burns were trading under another table, and a drunk, laughed Dorman beside them. Kenny Greene was with their self-proclaimed watchman.

Stroshine stumbled upon Mckenzie's table and only Mckenzie looked at him.

"Tonight I'd like a lay," he announced. "If I don't get another one my entire life, I'll take it."

Mckenzie did not know what exactly to say to this, so he said nothing. He watched the card game unfold, and when he looked up again, Stroshine was replaced by John.

"Come up to the bar," he said. The tips of his slicked-back hair were sprayed with the perspiration of the bar, and his fingers were red from the cold bottle in his hands. "Come get a drink."

Mckenzie thought about saying no, which he wanted to do, but when he couldn't think of a reason for it, he said he would. He slid his letter into his pocket. White slapped his back as he passed by him and his twirling girl.

"Rye! Come *party* with us." Brenner laughed, almost barking. He handed Mckenzie a half-finished beer, and Mckenzie accepted it grudgingly. He was enjoying keeping his head about him and seeing the others in such giddy states.

"To the old hell man himself," toasted Brenner, raising his whiskey above his head. "I'll bet his bloodied dick shriveled up in his hand at the last second."

He had a Star of David swinging around his neck on a chain. Mckenzie had never noticed it before.

John clapped him around the shoulder with surprising strength. His forearms were hot, his voice echoing and loud. "Hi there, I'd like a turkey club on rye please."

"Rye."

"Greene's all alone," coughed Mckenzie after taking a sip. It was not beer after all. "He's sitting there with that Colonel or whoever."

"Well then, he's not alone, is he?" John laughed again. An out-of-control laugh that Mckenzie didn't know if he liked or not. "Go tell him to get his ass over here."

"Tell him to quit sucking his mother's tit," said Vicky.

"The Colonel's tit."

Mckenzie did, trying his best to not look in the direction of the Colonel Whoever—as he was too able-minded for anyone else's comfort—and he hauled Greene over to the bar. His head was hung low. He was one of three boys who had not had a drink yet.

"Do you insist on not having fun ever, Greene?" roared Marshall, splashing the top of his drink onto Mckenzie's shoes. He felt a flash of irritation and would have shoved him a bit had it not been for his great mood. He was in a good mood.

"I'm having a time," said Greene sheepishly.

"He's here, alright?" Mckenzie interrupted. "Quit getting on his case." His stomach was feeling pleasantly warm after taking several gulps of his unknown drink and having John's arm hanging off his shoulder, his cigarette smoke flooding the inches in front of his face.

"Take a beer or something. Go get a girl," said Vicky.

"You get a girl," snapped Greene.

John and Marshall erupted with fits of laughter. John's hand hit Mckenzie's shoulder blades until he almost stumbled forward. "The comebacks tonight are just *out* of this world."

"I can get a girl," Vicky said.

Marshall pointed at a girl across the room sitting with three other girlfriends and whispering close to them. "Alright then. See her?"

"The red-hot fox?"

"Like Marshall himself."

"Yeah, that's the girl. Go talk to her. I don't know, go do something. Go fall to the ground and beg for her mother's hand in marriage."

"She's a pretty girl. Bet you can't get one of those," said Greene, who seemed to have become more comfortable after taking a shy look at his whiskey.

"No. I can. Choke on my success, Greene." And he marched over to the table of four girls. They watched the girls' conversation dwindle to a stop and the girls stare at Vicky. A minute passed with Joe shaking with suppressed laughter.

"Micky, I love you. I love this drink. I love life." John spread his arms wide to embrace the world.

"Shut the fuck up. I am trying to *listen*."

"Okay, well, you're not going to hear anything anyway; they're all the way across the room."

"Shut up, shut up, he's coming back!" John shouted. Vicky was slowly walking back to the bar with defeat.

"She's fucking forty," said Vicky solemnly. "You sent me to hit on a forty-year-old woman."

"Red-hot *fox*," said Marshall.

"You seem like the type to be into older women," Mckenzie said.

"She is not forty," said John. "Come off it. I have never in my nineteen years of life seen a thirty-year-old woman of that stature."

"She fucking told me I was too young. For Christ's sake, I could be her baby."

"You're my baby," John said sweetly.

"I'll shoot you when we get back."

Defeat, I assumed, made everyone a bit aggressive.

An hour had passed. The five boys retired to a table after the bartender cut off their drinks. He cut off their drinks because John demanded a naked blonde with a poodle under her arm with a lime on the side.

Lee was standing and talking to Mckenzie, who was sitting at their claimed table and could not hear him. John was passed out, his entire body weight leaning on Mckenzie's left arm, so he could not feel it very well, and he was snoring subtly in his ear. He was trying to hear what Lee was saying, but couldn't over the general loudness of the bar, the mumbling and yelling of the other men, Betchel calling out "Bullshit! Bullshit!" and John's liquor breath hitting his face so his cheekbone felt damp. He was actually feeling rather fuzzy, like his mind was too slow and his muscles weren't working correctly. His eyesight was blurry and his tongue was heavy on his teeth. He looked around at them all, took it in, and wondered who would be left when the days ran out.

20.

The Allies accepted Germany's first surrender in Reims, May 7th. The second was on May 9th in Berlin. Karl Dönitz was left to deal out the remains of possible winnings. Eisenhower cut the negotiations. And Stalin objected thrice. The ceasefire surrender of the 7th came into effect the next day at eleven p.m. with an extra minute. I watched the Londoners parade past Piccadilly. They held children over their shoulders and kissed each other on the mouths and held hands among the tangled crowd. They raised flags. They considered themselves to be the peak of nationalism until they considered how they had got here. They went home and left the last few stragglers stumbling past the bars and radio broadcasts. The highest points of the states joined in. Nazism broke. I witnessed a drunk celebrator fall into a trash can that night in the French Quarter. Nobody believes me when I tell them that, but I think you will.

The months have gotten shorter. I write to you at a time when the months have shortened to such an extent that as I close my eyes, I feel winter leaving behind its last breath. I can feel the decline of each season so the winter is a diminishing spot of cool land and fine-tipped leaves with the icicles crashing to the salt layered sidewalks. There is still snow. In parts of my vision, it is still red.

I write to you now in hopes that you will respond. You haven't yet. I expect you would rather focus on the writing itself. I reflect to you, only you, on my insecurities. I think about the past a lot. Sometimes I wake and think I am still there. I wake and feel lonelier than ever. I recollect on old conversations with those long gone. The souls I have lost. The ones that never should have trusted me. I believe it's safe to say that, at the time, I did not think anyone would get out of it alive.

-

Your pessimist.

21.

"*It's a* nice day out," June said.

"It's always a nice day here," Telly said.

It was, briefly and early, mid-May.

It was the day he received his first letter. It was the day I first thought of writing all this to you.

It was a Tuesday and his lessons had ended only shortly before. He was finding a favorite student in this one gal who slept through all his classes earlier than ten. Sometimes she would stay awake and tie her sneakers repeatedly in fun patterns. This amused him immensely.

Telly and June sat in the town square, on a bench in a small circle complete with a small bungalow and many pots of purple flowers. It was a fairly sunny, warm, and nice day. They had been sitting in silence for the first five minutes of their meeting up, and Telly did not know what exactly to say. He found he had nothing to say anyhow. Besides, the silence was not uncomfortable. Comfortable silence is the most at peace a person can be.

"What's that in your hand?" June asked suddenly, beckoning at his tight fist resting stiff on his thigh.

"Not much. Why do you ask?" He knew she did not believe that and he was not trying very hard to make it believable. Her milky brown eyes narrowed in a way that Telly could feel her biting at the corner of her wide lipped mouth.

"Let me see," was all she said and he opened his palm. In it rested a crumpled, yellowing envelope.

"A letter," June exclaimed. "From who?"

"This kid I tutored a few months ago. He's out at war now."

"Was he from here?"

"Yes."

"Well, I thought you can't be drafted here?"

"You can't," said Telly. "He joined up. He's not very bright. He's an excellent artist though."

She nodded and bumped their shoulders together. "My brother was drafted, you know. He's twenty-seven."

"I'm sorry."

She said, "That's the first time someone has had that response to his being drafted."

"What's his name?"

"Walker. He's got a little boy. Name is Clyde."

"That's sweet."

June told him that the war was ending in Europe in a matter of days. He suddenly felt lifted, as though someone was supporting the back of his head.

"Then Mckenzie will be coming home. He wasn't gone for too long after all."

"No. It's still going on in the Pacific."

"What do you mean, it's still going on in the Pacific? Why are we in the Pacific?"

"Japan," she said.

"We're at war with Japan?" he asked rather loudly. At that moment, a small group of older women passed by their bench and cast strange looks at them. June stayed silent until they were out of earshot.

"Yes," she said, quietly still. "We have been since Pearl Harbor."

Even Telly had heard of that. Although the town's draft laws had been in the books since 1862, brought back to life in 1937, Telly had heard about that. He remembered standing at the counter of the grocery store and seeing the cashier begin to cry. She was an older woman. He figured she was a mother.

"So he's not coming home?"

"No. I doubt he's even left to fight yet."

"Then what the hell is he doing?"

"Read the letter," said June.

He opened the envelope. First he noticed that certain words were blacked out. Then he noticed how the letter was addressed in Mckenzie's customary girlish cursive that took him ages to get through:

Dear loved one,

He did not address Telly. He said 'dear loved one' and that was all. The street name and number and town and state and country were correct, however. So Telly assumed that the letter was, in fact, meant for him.

Dear loved one,

I hope you've gotten this letter well. I decided not to sign your name so if the government thinks that you know too much, they will not be able to kidnap you. I am writing to tell you of our secret mission.

Actually, we have not yet left yet for ████. We are mostly waiting for news. I had my first real drink the other night. I know you were hankering on me about being a kid and I thought of you and I did it. I drank almost three things and got raging drunk and the next day we had off. I slept late and had a terrible headache, and you never told me about that part, did you? Adulthood comes with terrible headaches and I know that now. Thank you for not warning me.

They said Germany's cracking and I know that you probably don't understand that ~~because of~~ but I thought I'd say it anyhow so I seem like I know what is going on. Truthfully, I am pretty far behind everyone here because their fathers have all been on their asses to ship them off to ████ and I never even realized that was a place until a year ago. On the bright side, I have not started to pay taxes and whatnot, I have made friends, and I even had my first real conversation with a girl the other day. The day at the bar. She told me I was too skinny to be a soldier and John debated about punching her but then he realized you can't hit a girl. He said that girls are a lot smarter than the rest of us and if she said that I was too skinny, I probably am. John's a new friend of mine, and Lee. They've got the same funny accent as you.

I'm fairly well with doing whatever I need to do. Not so much that I'd become a target. I think I've become a lot smarter too, or now I am just understanding that I am smarter than I knew. I don't have much to say else, lest it get redacted. I'm sure most of this will be, because the military gets on your back about putting in important information. Sometimes it can get into the wrong hands. It is a need-to-know situation. Or maybe this letter is not very important in their eyes at all.

Mckenzie signed his name and nothing else. He had never busied himself with sentiments.

I was turning over a lot in my head that year, but mostly it was the same phrase, the only sentiment that Mckenzie had ever used in my presence. *Dear loved one*. It stuck with me for a very long time.

The next morning, Germany's surrender had been delivered.

22.

By the time Paris had opened their streets, it still did not matter. The boys were delivered to the Pacific in a matter of days, among the battered islands, the tangled roots of fallen hands nesting in the dirt clutching at their ankles.

They hustled out of the barracks, got together their gear, and became one group of men. They became one squad, and then an entire infantry division packed together. Transport ships were loaded. Mckenzie and his known foot soldiers were placed together for two weeks on water. They stuck by each other's sides. They made no new friends. They had no desire to.

The ships were fairly comfortable. Mckenzie recognized that they were similar to their old home with their yellowing bunks—closer together to fit the high number of men—and their eating habits were similar. He sat beside Lee and John, their group of friends dwindling to three. The group of men had found their dependents and it was too late to change by then. During peacetime, the ships held 2,200. By May it was 15,000.

John once woke Mckenzie up in the middle of the night. He was leaning over him, wide awake with a strange look of tragedy upon his face, so unfamiliar that Mckenzie could have reached for his bayonet. His ears were creased funnily, lips dried and cracked, his shirt smooth as though he had been sitting completely still for hours, and maybe he had been. Mckenzie asked him what the problem was. John leaned close to him.

"I can't sleep," he whispered. "I love to sleep but I can't right now."

"Just close your eyes," Mckenzie told him. Out of the corner of his eye, he could see Lee rousing and looking over drearily.

"I'm afraid to do that though." John gritted his teeth and he seemed very young, like he was informing his mother of the monster under his bed. "If I do that, they'll get us."

Mckenzie shook his head. He checked his watch. It was nearing three a.m.

"They can get at us while we're all sleeping," John conspired. It was as if he was a telling ghost story, his own.

"They won't," said Mckenzie, although he didn't have a clue who "they" was specifically and couldn't understand the threat in his tired state.

"They can just blow us up. Take the whole ship if they want to, if they catch us in their sight," he hissed.

"Stop talking like that," Mckenzie snapped.

"They don't sleep. They watch us through the peepholes under water."

"Shut up." And he considered popping him in the jaw for good measure. The old annoyance he had toward boys his own age was returning.

"That's pussy talk, Rye," said Stroshine across the room. He had been awakened.

"I didn't say it, John did," corrected Mckenzie, but Stroshine was already laying back down, and he did not respond. He sighed and turned back to John. He was actually shocked to see that the fearful expression was still on his friend's face.

"Go to sleep, John." He turned over on his side so he was facing Burns sleeping in a stiff position in the lower bunk to his left. He didn't hear John make another noise.

The next morning, he was shaken awake by Lee. "Come and get breakfast," he said. Mckenzie opened his mouth to give a greeting, but Lee was already stalking out of the room with Betchel. Mckenzie propped himself up in his bed and attempted to stretch his legs, but did not get too far as they hit something tough at the end of his mattress. He peered over.

John was curled up like a cat, like a child at the end of his bed. His hands were tucked under his chin. He was still sleeping. Mckenzie noticed for the first time that his under eyes were heavily pronounced in every shade of purple. He felt an intense wash of pity over his entire being and got out of bed, making sure to not wake the sleeper.

—

He spent the weeks on water balancing on one foot. He kept the other high in the air behind him and stretched his arm out. He shut this horribly old mind down and gave himself no time to think about how he felt. It was the impending doom of the islands knocking on his door. Something called the unknown. Something that I have explored only once. We completed these peculiar movements together.

One week on water and John was losing his mind. Mckenzie could tell. He asked Lee if John had some fear of the ocean, once again confronting that there were some things he would never know about the two. Lee said no. He said that his father was a fisherman and John liked to swim. Mckenzie asked if his father had died somehow and Lee said no. Both of his parents were stable.

He realized then that John was processing it the best out of them all. His brain was moving faster than the other men's, so quickly that he was already in the Pacific theater, on the beaches. John was filled with sand. If you looked closely, you could see it spilling from his ears. He was an excellent math student in his previous life and he had already calculated their chances of breathing upon American land again. He lay awake at night, all night, every night, and did math problems in his head. Mckenzie began to worry that if John was ever confronted by the enemy, he might stop and cry instead of kill.

Sometime in the last few days aboard the ship, Mckenzie stumbled upon an older officer sitting alone in the bunk room. It was suppertime. They were being shepherded out to the hall, but the officer was still sitting on his bed, looking at something.

"Supper," called Mckenzie, but the officer did not get up. He only turned toward the voice and smiled.

"Come here," said the officer, beckoning.

Mckenzie thought against this immediately. Earlier that week, just when he was sure his friend was feeling better, the soldier in the bunk beside John began whining one afternoon and would not stop until reinforcements were brought in. Then the soldier started to shriek that ants were eating the bottom of his feet and his cells were full of poison, so they took him away to somewhere where he could get some rest. When the whole ordeal was over, he turned to John and saw that he was rocking back and forth with his head in his hands.

Mckenzie's logic was that no sane man turned down supper. He did not want to be forced into a conversation with a crazy man and, worst of all, miss dinner. He was very hungry. It would be stupid to pass time by having a nice talk with a loony man.

He did it anyway, of course.

He cautiously went over to the man and stood a good ten feet away. The officer had his legs casually propped up on his bunk, his boots creasing the strictly made bed sheets, and a pad of paper in his lap. His large, kind eyes were fixed on Mckenzie. He couldn't have been older than thirty-two.

"Look what I've smuggled in," he said and held up the paper and a white, plastic rectangle. It took Mckenzie a moment to comprehend what he was seeing; a paper with blue spots on it and a watercolor set.

He felt full heartedly at ease in seconds and got closer without thinking about it. "Where'd you get those?" he said swiftly so the words jumbled together. Eagerness was thumping in his chest, his fingers were itching, if he could just reach out, he'd be there—

"This guy I know. He smuggled it in," the officer said happily.

Mckenzie took a closer look. The paper was not the kind he used at home. It was much thinner, yet coarser, so it almost calloused his fingers when he brushed them against it. The paint set had every average color of the rainbow, though the palette was bruised and dented and the colors leaked oil onto the glass covering, like oil on pavement. He marveled at the man.

"I'm painting the Pleiadian constellation," said the officer.

That was what the strange arrangement of blue dots had been. It had no air of sophistication and was nothing like how Mckenzie would have done it. But then again, he never saw the Pleiadian constellation. Perhaps it looked exactly like that.

For over half an hour, Mckenzie chatted animatedly with the man about painting. About art. For those minutes, he felt his old sarcasm coming back and he wondered when it had left him. He finally had something to say that was not vile or evil or disgusting or terribly truthful. He could say meaningless things for once and it would *mean* nothing at all.

The ship barracks steadily began to fill with men who were returning from dinner with full stomachs. Mckenzie stood up, frowning, and checked his watch.

"Shit, I missed dinner. I told myself I wouldn't miss it," he said aloud.

"They've still got some stuff there, I'll bet," said the officer. "If you get there fast."

"I'll do that," said Mckenzie. "Thanks." He did not know what he was thanking him for, but he couldn't say nothing at all.

"See you, brother." And the officer began to scratch at his painting.

Mckenzie pushed past the gaggle of soldiers yelling and talking, past the trio tossing a roll over the crowd of heads, and into the hallway. It was eerily empty, cold, so quiet that you could hear the hum of electricity, the kind he always heard at home.

"Hey!" a voice echoed, ringing against the walls of the empty hall. John appeared around the corner, waving a ham sandwich over his head.

"John."

"Where've you been? You missed dinner," said John agitatedly. "Now you only get leftovers from lunch."

"I was talking to this officer. He showed me this stuff he smuggled in somehow. Ham?"

"Yeah. You should have invited *me*, old pal," said John, but the normal teasing lilt to his voice was no longer there. It hadn't been there for the past few weeks. He stopped, leaned against the wall, then sunk to the floor. "It's quiet out here."

Mckenzie sat down beside him, wincing slightly at the freezing tiles. "Yeah, it is. How's Lee?"

"He sat with Betchel."

"You sat alone?"

"No." John annoyedly glared at him. "I didn't *sit alone*. My God, I sat with White and Vick."

"Alright, sorry."

"You know, I openly hate your guts," said John, spreading his arms. He clapped his hands together in his lap. "Eat your fucking ham sandwich."

Mckenzie moved his hand to take a bite. He didn't mention his slight distrust of ham.

Then John reached over and punched him in the nose.

Mckenzie stumbled back and instinctively pushed John to the side. His head bounced off the wall with a dull clunk, and Mckenzie gathered his hands around his face, feeling the blood begin to run through his fingers and into his mouth, pooling thick on his tongue.

He gagged, blinking away the sparks of light behind his eyelids.

"No, no, no." John clutched at Mckenzie's shirt. "Hey, wait, I'm sorry, I'm sorry, shit—"

His nostrils were stinging.

"Micky, look up, c'mon, I didn't mean it, tell me it's not bad."

It was a fairly upsetting hit.

Mckenzie coughed and wiped at his mouth, then at his nose. It was hurting like he had been in the cold for hours. He sniffed and recoiled at the blood in the back of his throat.

"What the *fuck* did you do that for?" Mckenzie demanded, and he shoved John's shoulder as hard as he could. The stupid guy didn't budge.

"I'm sorry, I'm sorry, I didn't mean it," he pleaded, and he began gathering up his shirt fabric, pressing it to Mckenzie's nose. "Just let me see how bad it is, c'mon, I didn't mean to—"

"You *fucking idiot*, what the fuck is wrong with you?" He pushed John back and then again and again, until he slipped and almost fell. Their faces were both covered in blood, and why did John have blood on him? He wasn't punched in the nose.

"I'm sorry, really, tell me it's not bad." John sounded like he might cry.

Mckenzie grabbed his shoulder and shook him, refraining from doing so too roughly. "You," he said, "Are a *goddamn idiot.*"

"I'm sorry," John said. And he let his head fall forward onto Mckenzie's shoulder.

Mckenzie's head was spinning with confusion. John was older than him. He was nineteen and he was always crying and Mckenzie wasn't, and here he had hurt Mckenzie and Mckenzie wasn't crying, John was the one being comforted, and to Mckenzie, it all felt so very backwards, so backwards that he had to check that the ground had not flipped upside down without his knowledge.

"I'm sorry," John mumbled. "I'm sorry, I'm sorry, I'm sorry."

23.

A town meeting had been called for the first time since '41. This meant trouble, if anything. It was requested by the spiting and conspiring boy-child-youths of the population. There was a ringleader among this band, a lieutenant, and a right-hand man. Telly recognized the latter as a kid whose older sister he tutored once for her freshman year. He looked over the group of boys and saw Mckenzie in every one of them. This statement he no longer used as an insult.

The meeting was hosted in the town hall by the diligent responsive board of town representatives. They organized pew-like benches for seating in rows among the hall, and by seven p.m., they were full. Tacked on the bulletin hanging on the right side of the room were old town photographs. The smallest was a caricature of Uncle Sam.

Telly was ten minutes late, but the seats had already been mostly filled. He sat in the last open one next to Rico, who was waiting patiently. Carrie was home with the kiddos. Rico said that he had left his wife in some kind of a state. She was mumbling about the town meeting, saying *I don't know about that law anymore*, deep in thought while holding her youngest child. Telly shook Rico's words off. Carrie was being ridiculous if she was doubting the safety of *the* law.

"What do you think this will be about?"

Telly simply pointed to the front of the room.

Six teenage boys were standing to the side of the board. They seemed at best indistinguishable from each other. Some were poised, leaning forward on their toes and falling back into place. Some cracked their fingers and others still whispered to each other, nervously overlooking the audience of muttering people. They were ready to pop the question; they were ready to risk it all. They had done their research, they had faced their parents and their peers and their little brothers with rounded shoulders, and they took their ideas from mankind's earliest predecessors, straight from the books. They had spent the past four years ignoring a war that was *happening*, possibly feeling left out of all the *excitement*, feeling that it was wrong to simply look away from the mess that was a war, just because they *didn't have to* be involved at all. They would live like cavemen for a while until somebody listened. Telly felt the resolve in the room growing by the second.

The conversation was said to be on town law, but that was so pityingly vague that everyone knew what the discussion would be about. The town was quite the same as every other town in the United States, whether the people agreed on this or not, and life's final knot would have been tied long ago had it not been for that one thing. That one final law. The drafting law.

Oh, how Telly had almost forgotten it. Suddenly he was remembering a February day when he greeted Mckenzie in town one weekend and saw how his eyes focused on the town hall, how dreamy he became, how his bones liquidized and melted into the snow! He should have known then that Mckenzie was no longer the town's; he would be something much more than anyone had anticipated.

"Can we start the meeting?" said one boy. He looked to be the oldest. Maybe eighteen. He looked vaguely familiar. Maybe he was one of the groupies who took the train to New York on Sundays and smashed ice bottles of bourbon on the sidewalks beside the library. They playacted adulthood most days and rolled cracking magnolia leaves into cigarettes to smoke in the basements before their parents caught them with their briefcases in hand. War, it seemed, changed people.

"Yes, yes," said a board leader. He stood up in front of the room while the other members stayed seated in the first row, and he looked them over.

"Good evening, everyone," he said casually. A few murmured replies made their ways to the front of the room.

"We've gathered here," he said, and Telly was reminded of a wedding ceremony, "to talk town rules."

"Law," corrected a board member.

"Law. Yes. We've had some talk coming to us from the younger generation—"

At this, Telly began to question what generation he himself belonged in.

Subtle whispers started up.

"Yes, yes. So of course the act of changing a town law would require weeks to process. We wouldn't be able to comply with these requests overnight—"

"I'm sorry," said a woman. "What law are we changing?"

"No, no. We're not *changing* it; however, there has been some talk—"

"Who's talking? I don't see why there should be a change if everything is going so very well," a man said. There was some applause at this.

"We're talking; we're changing it," the oldest boy said loudly, and his friends applauded their approval, but no one noticed. Telly found them difficult to understand. They wanted to go to war, they could! They didn't have to force *everyone else* to stare at the bloody massacres.

"What law is being changed anyhow?"

"Nothing has been approved *yet*—"

Was he the second youngest generation?

"Are we having a vote?"

"We are not changing *anything* at this time!"

"Are we voting now then?" Several people raised their hands.

"You haven't even heard what we are voting on," said the boy.

Second oldest?

"So we *are* voting."

"I vote for no change."

"What law is changing?"

"I'm sorry, when will this come into effect?"

Maybe fourth youngest. So the fifth oldest.

"Quiet, quiet!" cried the board member, wringing his hands effectively. The room hushed. Rico ducked his head down and dissolved into a fit of silent laughter.

"Shut up," hissed Telly, grinning widely. A woman and her children sitting in front of them were glancing around in an ostracized manner.

"We are taking into account the law created in 1862," said the board member, and when the boys showed signs of interrupting, he waved his hands indignantly. "Nothing, I repeat, nothing has been decided on. This is only a discussion on how the town feels about altering it slightly or completely writing it out."

The annoyed faces fell off.

"I don't mean to be insensitive," a young man said with a voice shackled with insensitivity. "But why the hell would we do that?"

There was no need for a basic statement. Formal speech was not formal here; they were born knowing every word to that law; they were to it.

"The war is *practically* over!" shouted someone. But Telly knew this could not be true, for Mckenzie was not home yet, or on the way home, so the war could not have ended. He was going to the Pacific theater to tramp around in the forest or on the beach or in the jungle. He did not know the expanse of the Pacific very well.

There was no need to be any more specific. They knew the law. The law knew them.

The boys had their arguments. But certainly, Telly thought, they would fall to pieces. They were too young; the littlest being, at oldest, fourteen. The fucking war would be over before *he* held a rifle. But there was always the next one.

24.

During nights when I insist on sleeping, I awake to nothing but bullhorns and a fiery allegory.

The covers are pulled up to my nose, the footsteps are in my ears. When I finally rip them off, I find no footsteps; I find no fire. I only see an empty black cave and remaining prints on the shore. They were here once, though it is hard to believe that now. I only believe in the noise that pushes me into consciousness, the dreams that tear my catcher.

I woke to nothing but bullhorns and fiery allegory for more than two years, and I will fall asleep to the sound of them for much longer.

—

The island was beautiful. That was the painful part, maybe. He didn't know. But it appeased his eyes, and their first view of it was through the circular windows of their vessel. Lee had elbowed him aside; he pushed to the front, his bored demeanor caving in as he pressed his pointed nose hard against the glass, so when he turned away, it was yellow under the skin.

Then John had his glimpse, and he didn't look longer than he had to. He broke free from the crowd of men, most of them the youngest the ship had to offer and waited alone for their interest to diminish. Mckenzie's left eye spotted a triangle of the window that was not being peered through and he got his another look of the Pacific this way; it was like a blurry vision of a postcard holiday island, and he thought of his parents. He had been doing a lot of that recently, thinking, most of it focused on his parents, some on his old friends whom he knew for sure he could beat now in a fight, some on home, and some on Lee and John. He felt that he was homesick for the first time in his life, and he understood the meaning. He was also beginning to feel that he was less selfish than he had thought. War sometimes does that.

It was one of the last days on the islands when it wasn't raining. It had been expected and predicted in the weeks before; the heavens would open up and the drops would tumble down until the terrain was one mass of slick, red mud, the mix of water and dirt becoming oil over peanut butter. But May's first weeks brought little of this. Days before, a soldier on the ship one night said aloud to his comrade that he could not sleep, for he would dream of the squelching sound of his boots in the Japanese ground. Mckenzie did not understand this fear very well at the time, but he thought of John anyhow.

"Plum rain's coming in," said Al as he looked through the circle window. "Can't tell now, but it is."

Lee explained to Mckenzie later that this term referred to the time of year when plums ripen in the historical belief that as the fruit fell, their moisture would turn to rain. He whispered it in his ear so the others would not hear; Lee feared their anger at the subject. The others didn't enjoy discussing the island the way Lee did. Lee loved thinking and talking about the curiosities in life. But the others weren't curious about the island at all.

The island was called Capital Island after a faulty translation. But the islands as a whole was a name Mckenzie had only heard in the last few weeks. He and Lee attempted to translate it completely, but it didn't work out. Eventually, Lee decided to split the word in two. He did this very incorrectly and came upon "Feeling," and for the second part, "Rope."

In weeks' time, Mckenzie would understand bits of Japanese and this would add to his disdain. He would hear a similar phrase before a Jap would kill himself in front of those who outnumbered him. *Tenno heika banzai.* Long live the Emperor. Once, he accidentally referred to Roosevelt as the Emperor. He corrected it. Then he realized that Roosevelt was dead anyhow and that Harry Truman was in office. He supposed these were all examples of Feeling the Rope.

Its real meaning was Rope in the Open Sea.

—

For a few days after docking, they were allowed to roam around a restricted section of the beach. The high-ranked officers were gathered together in blue beach chairs, the ones that could be put together easily, and they drank cold liquor from a cooler. They tilted their hats so they hovered over their left brows and looked very mysterious and calculating. The First and Second Lieutenants played games such as boxing with their hands tucked up in bubble wrap, so each hit made an amusing sound, and a game where one-against-one would knock the ball over the three-foot net to the other side. The other player would then attempt to hit it back with his foot and the game ended at twenty-one points, whoever was closest winning. John excelled at this game and earned the respect of one drunk Colonel who slapped him on the back and called him a pretty Yankee. John excelled at everything; he still did not smile.

John was drinking something out of a bottle. Throughout the day Mckenzie counted six in his hand. His ability to make friends under such ominous events was unmatched. He sat at the foot of a seated officer, a roaring drunk whose cup was lowering precariously over John's cap of gelled hair. The officers didn't seem much to notice John, but he had been invited over. He didn't seem to care; he brushed sand over his civilian clothes and pressed the cold glass against his lip until it was red. Lee watched him until he was tired. Then he sat with Betchel.

Late at night, Mckenzie found Lee and John sitting on the sand facing the water. He stood back and listened to them secretly. The drunk officers had retired to their rooms or bumbled around the beach drearily, but the beach was near empty. Mckenzie waited for them to notice him.

They didn't notice him. They appeared to be talking, but Mckenzie could not hear them. He caught fragments of their conversation. And John was crying. That he knew. He had grown used to the sound that John made when he was trying not to cry. He did it mostly at night.

Lee stood up suddenly and shook his entire body to get the sand off. Then he turned and left John sitting on the sand with his boots on the very edge of the Pacific. He met Mckenzie's eyes. He nodded his head and walked back to the ship. He was holding a half empty beer bottle by the neck and Mckenzie frowned, trying to decipher why this was a wrong sight, but then realized it was because Lee never drank.

By morning of their last day on the beach, something had happened. It had begun to rain.

It reminded him of a time when he was little. Maybe nine. It was raining the hardest he had ever seen it and his mother took him outside in rubber boots and they watched the worms scurry down the driveway. The dirt was overflowing from the flowerpots, and their white fence was speckled with brown raindrops. It smelled like wet tar. He had always loved that smell.

His mother tucked him up in a blanket after, a threadbare one that was a gift from his grandparents, and he pretended he was warm. It was before they had moved to town and before his father got that one, perfectly-fitting job, before he got nice glasses with the nice lenses and didn't have to squint to comment on how tall his son had gotten. He pretended he was warm and his father pretended he could see and they sat together, one family, and slept on their king bed until dawn came, and they awoke to a war empty of war.

25.

Eleven hours of prayers and then relief: The 29th of March, 1927, brought good tidings and a baby boy. The mother clasped her hands together. She had had the baby early, almost three months before the due date, but he had turned out alright. Very lovely.

She'd have to name him something special. The past few weeks had been unexpected. Tokyo had many banks and a portion were closing, their Finance Minister was thinking of a disaster from four years earlier. Katoaka was telling the news of the Watanabe Bank going "bankrupt." It was a shock and nothing more. Her husband told her there was more to come, and she believed him.

She would have to name her son something truly special. Her first boy. He would be her only boy, her only child. Here she was, holding him for the short moment she could, pressing his little body to her collarbone, and she was thinking of that earthquake. They had rebuilt their house since then, but her scar was still there. It was on the right side of her face. It happened when she heard that resounding impact four years ago and the plate she was assembling had splashed hot oil into the air. She decided to name him Kanto. Maybe it was fit for a girl, but it would fit him for now.

Kanto was eighteen and laying on the beach on his stomach. His torso and legs were spread out on the sand and his head was poking into the forest, his hands clutching at the bases of the Itajii trees. He was thin enough that he could not be seen unless someone was on his level. Grass was brushing his face in the tender wind. The mangrove land was alive with English speakers. He stretched his arm back to his pocket for the grenade.

Kanto was nearly nineteen and running at an American boy. He was a soldier raising his weapon. His finger pressed hard. It did not click into place. He was dark-haired and slightly big-nosed. Kanto thought he looked like every Anglo-American he saw the day before. The devil did not move his fingers. He got closer, both of them running and backing up simultaneously, until Kanto was but five feet away, with gun ready, and the American shot him. His last thought was of His Emperor, his mother, and an earthquake that hit the Kanto Region in 1923. He was ripped from life's womb. He was the devil's first kill.

26.

The new painting he was working on at the moment, was—it was the one.

Telly smiled at the thought. He brushed that vexatious slip of hair out of his eye. His black hair had grown in the past months. He hadn't gotten it cut since the barber shop closed; they had been receiving far too many out-of-town customers who became enraged upon learning the situation at hand. For now, there would just have to be a smear of red paint on his forehead, making his hairline look bloody.

But it wasn't just red, it was currant red, and it wasn't just a brush, it was scraps of an instrument invented solely for his hands. He could not understand how he didn't see it in the months before, how he must have walked about blindly with no hopes for his love! March began with landscapes and April was nothing at all but white, and now, May was a portrait with hand-selected swatches he had only seen in his dreams. He was painting a portrait of June.

It had all her sharp edges so far. The brown for the hair would be the perfect color, and the curvature of her hands were set beside reality. It was realistic, but not too docile, dreamy and picturesque and grounded. It was the best thing he had crafted before, and he had no desire to burn it or throw it away. That was a first for him. Maybe, he thought impulsively, he would become better than Mckenzie. But he shoved the thought away. How selfish one had to be to believe that, he did not know. All he knew was that he no longer woke in the middle of the night from garish dreams of lucid, milky colors coating his fingers, and hazy, dark figures waving from the peripherals of his vision. He would sit up in bed and look around his room, demanding the kaleidoscope of shapes make any sort of sound, make anything at all, and they never did. Now he no longer had to ask.

Besides, Mckenzie was off his talented track. The wheels spun in the middle of some strange jungle or beach. He had a gun and a bayonet now.

He was probably starving, Telly thought. But he pushed that thought away, too.

—

Carrie dropped by Telly's that Friday night. She found him sprawled on the living floor beside his easel, listening to the radio. The President was talking to him.

"Hello, Harry," she said. She was wearing a nice dress and her husband's winter overcoat. It had been a cold day.

"Ah." Telly leapt up and greeted her gallantly. "I've got a big brain for you today. I've really been working hard and I think I've got somewhere at last. I may die from the shock of finally completing a project, but, God, what a way to go out!"

"You're excited," she said.

"I guess I am."

"You'll freeze if you keep the heat off in here," Carrie scolded.

"The cold gets my brain moving. It wakes me up. I am more productive. It's very cold for May, isn't it? What the hell's going on today, huh?"

"It's fifty-four."

"Fifty-four. Jesus."

"Let me see your painting."

He showed her. It was propped on its easel and recharging for another day.

"So that's her?"

"That's who?" he humored.

"Your girlfriend. Girl who's a friend. June."

"Yeah. She's wonderful to paint. I don't even have to have her right there in front of me; I can just see her in my head."

"It's marvelous. Great."

"It is, isn't it?" Then he promptly remembered to be modest. "Well. It's not much, really.

"I've got something to talk to you about," said Carrie.

Telly ushered her over to the lumpy sofa. It was cold, the same kind of cold the day was leaving as reminders. He was never using the sofa anyhow; he'd rather collapse himself completely on the floor to keep his mind roaring.

"We'll talk," he said. "What should we talk about?"

"For starters, we're moving."

If possible for May, it got colder.

"Moving?" he repeated sluggishly.

"To Philadelphia."

"Philadelphia?"

"Yes. It's west of here."

"Philadelphia's outside of town."

She smiled. "I know. But it'll all be over soon. In a few months, I'm sure."

"Yeah, it'll be fine. Until the next war."

"You're mad at us."

He thought of repeating his words to Mckenzie. "No. I'm not mad."

"You're just going to miss us, then?" she asked hopefully, giving an understanding smile.

He shook his head. "I don't understand why, all of a sudden, everybody is so very quick to get out of town."

"Mckenzie's eighteen," said Carrie gently. "You can't blame him for that."

"I wasn't talking about Mckenzie." His throat was closing up on him, but he wasn't crying or yelling or particularly angry. "I don't understand why, all of a sudden, people want to change the rules."

"You know this country was supposed to have special privileges for none?" she mused.

"Well, that's a lie. *Tons* of people have special privileges. Nobody wants to get rid of those. But, of course, we just love war and killing people and fighting with foreign countries, and when someone offers a small solution, everyone tears it down."

She was quiet.

"You're really running away from something that does absolutely *no harm* at all! What happens when some politician gets pissed at another in fifteen years and Frank has to go off?"

"Telly," she interrupted.

"There aren't any downsides to this life, Carrie! We're safe. Compared to everyone else."

"We're mindless," she snapped, "We aren't doing our part one bit. We've forgotten about the people who *don't* have this privilege. You're forgetting about—"

"Mckenzie *had* that privilege—"

"I wasn't going to *say* him. I was going to say Rico's brothers."

"His brothers?" A sense of nostalgia hit him. "Jesse and Marvin?" he recalled, like it was yesterday, sitting in Rico's office, listening to him rant on the going abouts of the country, accepting his brothers' fates, and how Telly sat there, letting each word pass in and out, and feeling nothing at all. March was an alien lifestyle; in March, they were babies.

"Yes." She stepped forward, her mouth of steel stretched tight. He felt a lecture coming on. "They died for this country, you know. They had to go. They had no choice. And we pretend that that is a thing of the past."

He shook his head, almost laughing.

"You can't change the past. It is what it is," she said.

"We were supposed to learn from it," he raved.

"Maybe we will next time. You can't control when they understand."

"You think there will be a next time?"

"I think it will be different next time. I can't imagine this having no effect at all."

"You know," said Telly. "Sometimes I picture this scenario where Mckenzie comes home. And he sees nothing has changed and everyone is going about their lives as if he never left. And he is completely different."

"It could happen."

"I was thinking about that at the town hall meeting. The other night. And I was thinking, well, how is he going to live with that? He went off to war and no one cares because no one knows. I don't even know."

"So you're understanding what I'm saying."

"I believe so. But, I have a hard time saying that. I guess I was much happier when I had special privileges."

"You still do," Carrie said, and she began to fiddle with his fireplace.

"I don't feel as though I do. I know a fraction of what there is to know and I was thinking Mckenzie knows so much more than I. How could I compete?"

"Compete?"

"How could he ever come back here?" asked Telly, folding his hands in his lap. "There's nothing here for him anymore."

Carrie looked him deeply in the eye. He suddenly felt as though he was being x-rayed.

"If we change the law, a lot of people will die someday," he continued. "And yet—"

"Don't worry about the law anymore," she said, "That is someone else's problem. It sounds quite selfish to say, but it is. Somebody made that law hoping for it to never come into action. We must deal with the remains."

He nodded. Carrie always spoke so nicely to him.

"And you must know," she said, "Every one of those boys is a hero. Whether they asked for it or not. Your friend is."

"He's not my friend. He's a repugnant little beast who pesters me on my teachings."

"That is only something you would say about a friend," Carrie presumed, grinning. "I think you should paint him. Like how you did June."

Telly considered this. He looked at his easel. "I wouldn't want that hanging around in my house. I'd have to give it to him. And I wouldn't be able to. I don't think he's coming home after all this," Telly said.

Carrie sniffed. There were pricks of tears in the corners of her eyes and Telly didn't know why. "I don't think he is either," she said.

27.

In his nightmares, it was always dark. But this day, he woke up and it was too bright. He looked at John. John was looking back at him. The skin under his eyes was pink. It was dirty too. His nose was peeling. His tongue was dry, and Mckenzie knew this because everyone's was; his own was. John's lips were sunburnt. Mckenzie was wishing for a cold day in May. By night, he dreamed of leftover sandwiches and dry skin. By day, he never slept.

"My face hurts now," said John.

It was almost June.

—

It was an impenetrable jungle when he was stuck there, when they packed up and moved off the beach, one long line of men staggering into the tropic, festering on the last bits of their drunkenness. Okinawa was lengthened sixty miles; it stretched less than nineteen miles wide. The north was a terrain of thick forests and hills. The south was farmland. Its ridges and cliffs lined the path to Shuri, the pastoral land decorated with the elaborate tombs of the Japanese's dead. The Americans smelled the pine that lingered. It smelled, for some, of home. Past the beach, words of caution came to the mind of soldiers at the jungle rot and the habu snakes. They had been warned by the men that came home fresh from the island and when they were not there to warn the next group, I would be the warner. The Marines subdued the north; the regular Army was going south. The Marines were decorated risk takers. The Army planned to operate with their typical deliberate passiveness, their heavy artillery fire, and their reinforcements making the trek through the jungle to their positions. The first hour they sang sailor songs. Mckenzie thought of an old friend of his from school; old because he had not spoken to him since before his birthday; a friend because of his gift for singing, something he only pulled out on special occasions.

Once, on one of their first nights, Mckenzie lay awake and saw a flying chrysanthemum leer over him in the air. He fell asleep before hearing its destruction. They all saw the planes. They all said nothing. You do not mention the taboo.

Operation Iceberg was not cold. Perhaps it was silly to hope that it would be. Naha was taken on the 27th, and yet still, they were walking. They were pushing forward. But the sun was burning the whites of their eyes, or its shine was completely blocked, with no in-between. It was one of the last days of May. Imperial Japan was falling. And yet still, they were walking.

Mckenzie was calculating his height that morning. They were waist-deep in slick mud, and the torrential downpouring pressed them further into the ground until their ankles were hurting with the pressure of holding themselves up. Some of the men were up to their chest. The mud smelled almost refreshing, earthy and rich, reminding them of summer rain. When Mckenzie's company had approached the first signs of mud, one soldier stepped forward confidently, only to fall with his hands out to shield himself. His comrades pulled him out of it, steering clear of the path. It took days for his uniform to harden into a crust of removable dirt. He said later that he thought he was drowning. The memory of it was strong enough in his mind for him to paint a picture of it.

So he was calculating his height, trying to determine what percent of his body was submerged. He continually scraped the mud off of his front teeth with his tongue, the thick mixture lathering itself to his molars until he tilted his head back to reach for the rain. John was maybe the tallest of his squad, the one that they began with, with Mckenzie and Lee and John and Marshall, the Halsteds, Greene and Betchel, Sid Dorman and Burns, and White and Stroshine. Forrest Burns had been sent to join another company before they left the beach. He died behind lines running supplies to the front with white phosphorus shells coming down to Earth.

Sergeant Travers was behind the squad of leftovers. Sometimes he muttered to himself. But the night before, while Mckenzie was waiting for the suicide planes to fly overhead, he heard Travers whistle. The whistling only made his overstimulated ears pang worse. Mckenzie would turn to his right as they walked, and there was Lee, his owl eyes hardened to brace against the erosion blowing into their faces, and he would turn left, and there was John, his chin tilted downward, watching how his body continued to push through the mud, looking carefully to see if the lifting of each leg was visible to the eye.

"I'd like to be a Seabee now," said White from somewhere behind Mckenzie.

"No you don't. You don't wanna get tossed overboard, pirate," said Al.

"I'd welcome that." He cracked a smile and his gums were white. "I'd like to go for a nice swim right about now."

"Go dive in the deep end," said Lee and he gestured to the clay. John snickered.

Mckenzie balanced himself as best as possible and dropped his head back, letting the warm rain run down his face, into his nostrils and mouth. "It feels like blood, it's so warm."

"What does?" asked Lee.

"The shit."

"Be careful up there," John hissed to Brenner, who was closest to the front. "There's a man who's got bug eyes." He was less humorous than the words offered.

Mckenzie craned his neck. He could see a veteran from Peleliu with his arms around two others. His face was near yellow.

"His face ain't as bad as yours, John." Al giggled.

Mckenzie looked at John. The skin on his shoulders were damp and pickled; he was red from the days with sun. Al smiled and Mckenzie felt a twinge of annoyance.

"Shut up," he said. He had been saying that a lot recently. It felt like a part of his old vocabulary.

Within the hour, they had stopped to eat. They passed whatever was left of the C-Rations and some new stuff, a mixture from a Guadalcanal warehouse. Mckenzie cursed the men there who had not picked out the insects. But he did not either. He kept one hand on his weapon and the other dipped into the tin, flicking away any rotting vegetation that fell into his food. He ate ravenously. When he had finished, he turned to Lee, who was still eating. He watched him intently.

"Someone's throwing," said Lee. They looked ahead. It was the veteran from Peleliu with malaria.

"He's wasting it," said Al.

Mckenzie again was hit with the briefest surge of anger, which relaxed when he saw John rolling his eyes. Mckenzie winked clumsily at him and tried not to feel the mud leaking into his Army-issued shirt; lately he was feeling as though he and John had switched roles.

"Hey," Dorman said. He swallowed his grub and picked a bit of rubble from his teeth. "Where do you think Forrest is?"

"Listen, Burns is probably at some field hospital with his ass in a sling listening to Jack Benny on the radio. He's not—" White's voice cut out a moment and then he reappeared, his white hair growing brown. "Who's the guy saying he's off to Guadalcanal?"

"That was me, White," said Dorman.

"He's not in Guadalcanal, you fuckhead."

"I heard they've got bad grass there," said Green.

"The Yamatos with the Coke-bottle glasses are getting bad highs?"

"No," said Green. "They have this grass. I heard another man up front talking about it. They call it Kunai grass. It grows right up to your neck and it's sharp. Like a knife kind of sharp."

"Good thing Burns isn't there," said John. He took out his canteen, looked at it for a moment, then licked his lips and put it away.

Mckenzie patted through his gear. "My bedding's wet."

"So's the rest of ours. It was last night."

"No, I know. But it's worse today."

"It rained less today," said Lee.

"How can you tell?" said White.

"From a scientific standpoint—"

"I don't really care, Collins."

"Hey," said Mckenzie. When nobody heard him, he said loudly, "Hey! What's going on up front?"

They all heard it then. Gunshots and yelling and strange screeches and the sound of adrenaline running. The line backed up and Mckenzie stumbled, reaching for his rifle.

"Alright, alright," murmured White and he narrowed his eyes, waiting patiently for something, anything, to come into sight.

They had their weapons positioned, ration cans quickly discarded and stashed for later. Mckenzie wiped the sweat off his forehead, nudging his helmet.

He waited for something to kill him but nothing did.

For now, however, he would be content with nicking trees and elbows. His breathing shuddered, his finger hovered over the trigger, and he had a brief nightmare of knocking the rifle out of position and accidentally pressing the trigger, and shooting John down. His heart was beginning to hurt in his chest, his fingers itched to go, and he thought, No matter how bad fighting is, it won't be as bad as the waiting. He was not yet a suicidal man.

28.

There was whispering among the living about one who wouldn't live any longer. He was a bit older than Mckenzie, hopeful to live, because a shot anywhere other than the heart or head meant a trip to a hospital, and maybe home. But the man was dead. He had been dead for quite some time, the others not knowing exactly what to do with him. So they left him there when the first skirmish was over. They endured the next combat, and the next. Still the man's body was there. Another group of men were marking up maps some few feet away. Mckenzie slowly sipped at his canteen. A soldier across from him with a bloody ear did the same. Mckenzie's canteen was nearly empty. The last wave of fresh water had come up the beaches and into the jungles a week before their arrival. And now they were needing creativity. He wasn't dreaming of home. He was dreaming of a sweet, cold glass, and now this was a problem. Wounds weren't the issue; not every man was affected. But every man, every human, could not sustain the lack of sufficient water without their brain cutting off chief wires.

He baited his desire by trudging through the mud back and forth, retrieving needed items and passing around the plan, the places they needed to get to, the things they needed to conquer. He spent his last hours of sunlight talking over plans with Travers, whose tough skin was hardly bearing winter's crack. Mckenzie pushed his thirst further back and still it inched faster than his feeble, weakening feet could handle. He thought he possessed a handle over his body. But the thirst creeping in was more than he could power off. He grew jealous of the other men, those who were taught properly how to ration, something he had somehow missed. He became annoyed at the zeal often worn by the men with stronger arms than he. Already some were hungering for something they could not reach. One night, Mckenzie woke and found that the relieving water on his tongue was nothing but the rotting imaginary blood and the sour leftovers of a bombardier, the fiery flesh dying on his lips. He yearned to hand the gift to someone else.

So it was slow at first. And he found himself thinking that the run with death could grow on him.

Lee was sitting beside him, cleaning his rifle with a sleeve. He was always cleaning that rifle; regardless if his entire body was filthy, he cleaned that gun. The bullets were clean.

He polished it at best he could, sitting down in the mud, the bottom of his boots crusted over. He didn't go over their new plans. He and Mckenzie listened to their orders and took them on and understood them as best they could, and they never spoke of them again. Perhaps they were too difficult to voice aloud. Their understanding was far and few. Mckenzie studied Lee's careful conduct of his weapon. It was raining, the water dirty and almost refreshing, and it slipped down his neck and into his shirt. He stretched his taut muscles.

"Did you wanna hear a funny thing?" he said.

Lee nodded, scratching at the dirt on his jaw.

"Okay," he said. "Well, I've got this friend."

"I'd hope so."

"And when he was really young, he decided one day that he would just pretend to be invisible. And see what people would do. So he ignored when people tried to talk to him all day long, and then he decided to do it for a couple of days. And his mother thought he was going deaf, so she brought him to the doctors. And the doctor said there was nothing wrong with his ears, so they go home and his parents are begging him to speak, and he's starting to feel bad about it. So the next day, he wakes up really excited and marches up to his parents' bedroom, opens the door, and yells that he's alright, that he can talk and all. And his mother frowns, really confused, and says to her husband *hey, did you hear that*? And she slammed the door shut and the door knob hit him right in the eye. So he got this scar right below his eyebrow."

"Did that really happen?" Lee said.

"No. Did it sound really unrealistic?"

"Kind of."

"I do have this friend though. And he did have a scar below his eyebrow. I just don't know where he got it."

"What's his name?"

"Telly."

"Weird name."

"Yeah."

"Tell me about him," said Lee, and he set his rifle down.

29.

June was coming. I warned you about incoming storms before. I told you before April and May began. I give you, for the second time, a look into myself. If you've ever believed, I'll tell you another story. I wish to be yours truly, your beloved holder. I unhook your faithfulness; I tether myself to you.

I was born in the darkest of places. I remember my earliest nights, when I never had to brave twilight, how they comforted me so and led me to reconciliation. They held my hand. They fed me and when I could not be fed any longer, I fed them. I looked down upon them all and smiled. I understood unconditional and requited love.

The years passed by; they grew talons. Their love was complex and dirty. They demanded my love and showed what they had done for me. I retreated away. They were thinking too much of me, or not at all. They were not thinking of their fellow creatures. They said they loved me and yet never wanted to know me. I was their creator and they fell to my feet and covered their ears.

And still there were the ones who I never felt this way with. I could sit by and listen to them for hours and they never asked any more. They listened to me. And one by one, they fell. Disappointment broke their wings; they were killed and taken and bothered and forgotten about. Suddenly nothing was all they had and it was not enough. I held empty promises and *nothing* more. I made verses with the dead and they sent me to the living. I covered my eyes; I couldn't look at them because I saw myself. I wished to speak their language, for few of them spoke mine. I was never upset when after a few tries of talking to me, with no response, they stopped talking altogether. I understood it. I was doing the same.

In retrospect, looking back, I hated myself. There was no building I would not have flung myself off of, no depth of Hell I would not succumb to. I told myself that I would make it up to humanity. But, there was never enough time. I was patient around the clock and suddenly, I realized that I had spent my waiting minutes speaking only to those akin to my being. It was all a waste of time. I, their creator, was debating on destroying it all. I wanted to take myself out of the world, but I could not; I was not my own maker. They gave me that title and there was absolutely nothing I could control. But there came a time when this mindset began to change.

Yes, they named me their creator, and I thought I broke every single one of their hearts. It wasn't their fault. They could not help their misunderstanding of me, even when tears froze and melted to their faces, and each morning, when they woke up, found their limbs were cold and numb for a few moments longer than the last day. It was deeper than feeling a hand on the shoulder when no one is there, deeper than speaking to me and getting a spoken response. I *was* the heart of the people. I was their stories and their friendship, and they brought me into treacherous terrains, into smoke filled air and broken formations, and they let me fly free, urging me to find the good in the place humanity had built to ruin themselves. I thought I was their downer. I thought that I had disappointed an entire race of beings, but maybe they had disappointed me.

So I warn you one last time, my friend. My dear loved one. I tell you to tread lightly and I don't ask you to blindly hold out your hand to me. I could tell you that I am always watching, but this isn't true. My job is not what you say it is. I have paved my own road and I will do this onward. Do not pray to me; I pray for you.

After everything, I still wish I could change the events that took place that month.

June 1945. It was almost over.

June.

4

Carrie left. Telly sat in front of the fireplace and fell asleep there wearing his thickest socks and a blanket. He woke up on time without having set an alarm.

He dressed and readied himself to teach, and because he was strangely attentive, as he had not been in the past few weeks, he managed to drive himself to his class without difficulty. He stopped at a stop sign instead of rolling it.

He was late of course, because of his good, lawful driving and because he woke up at the intended time forty minutes before class started, and because he lived half an hour away from the building. He threw his belongings on his desk at his arrival and looked toward the seats. They were filled with his usual students, who were looking too preoccupied to notice him even entering the room. He gave a sigh of relief that his tardiness would not result in a layoff.

The students, all fifteen of them, as the numbers had curiously dwindled since the start of 1942, were crowded around a radio. Another one. It was resting on one girl's claimed desk, and she sat back in her chair with a look of hostility toward anyone who accidentally jostled her area of Zen.

"What's going on?" Telly said, and when none of them answered, he shouted, "Alright, time for that big test!"

They looked up. Fifteen twenty-year-old faces, varying between worry, confusion, and satisfaction.

Okay, thought Telly. *What the fuck has happened* now?

"Hey, where's Marcia?" he said, scanning his audience. "She out today?"

There was silence. Then one boy said, "She dropped out."

"Out of what?"

"… Her classes."

"Oh. I didn't get her letter."

"Maybe she didn't send one."

"I guess not."

Telly frowned. "What's on the radio?"

"They're talking about the camps in California," said a boy.

"He doesn't know what those are," whispered another, but loud enough that Telly could hear it.

"Does this happen to have anything to do with the war?" he said. "Or Marcia?"

—

He was sitting alone in his office, reviewing the previous lesson. He was teaching surreal art, in which he went through paintings in Europe after the first war. The class looked at a lot of Salvador Dalí and spent some time on the Henry Ford Hospital.

Telly was planning on having them write some sort of short statement on one of the pieces they had observed. They were good kids, the whole clan of them all. He was turning over The Great Masturbator, thinking about his intelligent students, and began to think of what they had told him. He thought of Marcia, and how she liked oddly named paintings, and passed in her own pieces with such strange titles. He thought of this with an uncomfortable feeling, like he was thinking of a ghost.

They had been listening to a government official speaking about the relocation. The Japanese relocation, of more than a hundred thousand people of such descent dropped off in camps. The radio specifically was talking of one camp in California. His students told him most of the relocating was being done on the Pacific Coast. They also informed him that Marcia was, in fact, Japanese. Telly hadn't felt so—there was no other word for it—*left out*, when he heard this. But he reminded himself, the *left out* feeling was good. He wouldn't want to be surrounded by a war that caused destruction in the safe places, too.

Her parents were owners of a gas station until they were not. Actually, up until recently, they had been living comfortably with their business, and sending their daughter to a class close by. She never missed Telly's class. He intuited what had happened through the students talking over one another, that Marcia had come home one day and found her parents with less money than ever and no business. Her classes were only extra weight.

Telly looked through the last assignments he had given out that were just turned in. He turned over in his head the idea of surreal art and having a favorite student, until they became one blended idea, until he could see Marcia sitting in his class with her pen poised, and one hundred extensions of herself attached. He picked up the telephone and dialed a number.

"Hello," he said. "Yes, hi. June, let's go out tonight."

-

June was barely eleven when her father came home with no weekend checks. She was almost twenty-two when Pearl Harbor was attacked.

She grew up in a sunny town. She attended elementary school with her older brother and swam the beaches on Sundays. She played hopscotch on the sidewalks and waited for more money. I did not know her in those times, and she briefly knew me. She met me for the first time in a side street booth, where two middle-aged women were selling my story. Her brother often put me down. When he did so, it was always at the dinner table when there was not much for dinner. He'd be sent to their room, without a bite to eat, as their parents said, and June would think that staying at the table would not bring much to eat either. She poked moodily at her paltry meal.

She dated a small group of boys whom she did not have much interest in. It was not that there were any problems with them, or herself. She simply could not find one who took her attention entirely off the situation at hand. The situation being the state of her home and family, the town and state and region, the whole country and the whole world, and my God, her brother was truly in some deep water these days. He stole often. He must have taken his parents' words to heart, for he ate alone, outside, and all of it was stolen. So, quite honestly, her dates and friendships revolved around little talking and more of looking out a window and creating funny, satirical jokes to explain the next crisis that had disrupted her life. Whatever was supposed to be in the world of a teenager, June figured she was lacking it.

She took up the job at the diner because they were hiring and for no other reason. This was no complication of fate, one that I took her up on and created this opportunity for her, one where she meets the protagonist of my stories. In fact, I had never seen her before. She was not usually the type to go to church, and if she was, I didn't find that one special chapel. Instead of praying, she earned her tips by being downright humorous or being interesting enough that she piqued the minds of every customer. She had funny, unusual tales and ones with lessons in them, too. And she was a wonderful liar. Somedays she would tell events that had never happened before in the history of humanity, and still she would make it believable, until she believed it herself. The day she met Telly, she could not help the lying. Yet, she liked how easily someone could understand her by only hearing her name.

It was hurtful to admit, but June knew she never had a storybook life. Nearly nothing in her day was curious, as it had happened to everyone. Everyone's father was running out on a job. Everyone's older brother was behaving awfully. Every girl was sick and tired of it. Everyone took up smoking, though she was sure that she was the only person who directed the smoke up, so as not to get in a person's eyes. She enjoyed how Telly marveled at that attitude. It made her feel like she was not every single person destroyed by a decade wrapped in one body.

She liked how she looked. She thought it made her seem more trusting and possibly funny. June believed that funny people were hardly drop-dead beautiful, and while she wasn't ugly, she wasn't shocking. Her looks were just right enough so that they furthered her personality. She tried her best to always enhance herself deeper into the kind of girl who was never affected by anything. She lied habitually about unimportant things. Her lies made her better.

When Pearl Harbor was attacked, she was at home with her parents with the radio turned on like every other almost twenty-two-year old girl. She did not hate the unison then. At that moment, it comforted her. Her parents cried and held hands and their breakfast went cold. When the crying was done, they ate the cold food instead of getting more when they could have, when they had the resources to. She watched her parents sit close together in the living room, her on the opposite side. It had been a year since her brother's death and she was still leaving room for him on the sofa.

I couldn't account for her life after the war. I saw her last at the end of summer, 1945. I did not see her until she was gone. She had never talked to me before, and her brother had gone out himself cursing my name, but she knew me. She found me very easily.

One humanly summer day, she came to me along with a group of others. She was making friends with the young and stepping strongly into my presence, where others were cautious.

God-fearing, I said.

But I knew her. She was old now, and it was years later, when there had arisen a new kind of land and language of politics, a new way of lying, and June understood this. She understood that I immediately recognized her.

Do you know me? she said.

You know I do, I said.

Mind telling me how? she asked me with a grin on that wide mouth.

I told her no. And I told her that I had someone she should see. An old friend, I said. After all, it really had been a number of years. And this friend was a memory I had never lost track of.

God-fearing, I said.

What's that? June said.

Oh, nothing, I said. *Come. Let me bring you to Telly.*

31.

The Peleliu vet was gone before the day's end. He was shot fast. They left the scene as quick as possible to cut off the malaria. He did not have many friends in the infantry. His old comrades from Peleliu had long left him, and he them. Overnight, shrapnel was falling. The high-speed rush of planes overhead was rustling the trees, making the steady leftover rain drip down.

It had been a few weeks. Maybe two. They were mostly lucky through the night. Their beginning group was stable except for Jack Betchel.

He was hit in the hip by *something*, which Lee attempted to determine, but he was pushed away by Jack. Jack shook his head at John and brushed his fingers gently over the wound with a grimace.

"I'll be alright," he said. "I'll get it cleaned up soon."

So they waited for the supply jeeps to turn up and take him to town. Mckenzie bent forward and dragged his palm over his face. He was shaking. He felt very much like he was wearing no clothes at all, as they were soaking in saturated sweat and dirt against his skin. He was entrenched in mud. It was drying around his ears.

"Your ear's bleeding," murmured John. He reached over to Mckenzie, his gun slinging back and forth. He held his hand outstretched without touching, like an Egyptian. Mckenzie felt at the back of his ear.

"No, your other ear. Other side."

He touched his left ear. The hot liquid was still damp and the dirt on his hand smudged into the nick. He winced slightly.

"Does it hurt? Let me look." John forcefully turned him around and then more carefully traced the pattern on the cut on the back of his ear.

"You got nicked by a bullet," said John. He let go of Mckenzie. "You'll be alright. It'll clear up."

"It doesn't hurt," Mckenzie lied. He pressed his sleeve to attempt to stop the bleeding, so the blood would not flood his nostrils in his sleep. It was a pretty color. He noticed, even if no one else did, that everyone's blood was a different color, something strangely dissimilar set against the canvas. "How's Betchel?"

Jack was leaning against Dorman and Lee, the latter of whom was passing dirty bandages to him. He motioned for Jack to show him the wound. It was at the very bottom of his side, the top of his hip. The blood was brighter than anything they had seen in a while, and Lee wiped the small hole with wrapping. The skin around it was steeped in the ooze of the land, festering and irritated under his soaked clothing.

"Bugs will get at that," said Al.

Someone was throwing up.

The ground tilted under Mckenzie's feet, and he lurched forward, and he felt like very-real hands were tearing at his eyeballs and plucking his nails out one by one, and pressing his shoulder blades into the ground, and he was crying. Terror was crashing over him.

"Are you okay?" John asked.

"Yeah," he said. "Give me a moment." For five minutes, he was bent over, screwing his eyes closed against the mud and the strain of malaria mosquitoes flickering against the tree roots. Then he pulled himself up.

"You've got blood all over your face," John muttered, looking up at the sky.

He wiped it off with his sleeve.

—

Betchel was infected and the jeeps weren't there. They could not even hear them approaching. The entire company was halted, and the dead Japs littered the ground uphill, the rest of the living ones having retreated backwards. They were completely landlocked.

Jack Betchel was leaning back against a tree and not accepting any help for his injury. He smiled with a careless loss of energy, his strong form receding into an unhealthy pallor, and Lee hovered by, tapping his fingers rhythmically. Mckenzie watched him confusedly, until remembering the days when he and John sat together in silence, and how he had never wondered where Lee was. Looking back now, he saw Lee and Betchel, the only two who did not drink, the only ones sober, the earliest risers, the ones Travers had liked the most. He recalled the first time he had seen the logical man of the group, green-eyed and muscular and married, and how he had told them about his children. He had his wife and his children and still he was not accepting help. He waved away the morphine and the plasma, repeating that the supply jeeps would come sooner or later and take him off to the village, then fly him to Guam. He pointed his thumb to the front, where a strange, ghostly groaning was coming from. The medics passed him and moved down the line. And Mckenzie remembered that Betchel said something he could not hear and smiled at him. *He* smiled at *him*.

When the jeeps came, they parked nearest to the Jap's line of defense and picked up the injured there. They drove past Travers and Dorman, Mckenzie and Lee and John, Sammy Brenner and the Halsteds, Marshall and Stroshine and William White. Lee was no longer pacing and his peacefulness was unnerving Mckenzie; John, for once, was not crying.

32.

The second day of June in the Pacific irritation. It brought Al swearing at Dorman on account of his hearing abilities; the rain was shells and perspiration the night before. Joe Marshall was complaining of a foot infection.

The second day of June brought two new faces. Mckenzie killed his first man on this day.

—

Henry Eubank was the commanding Major in the company ahead of theirs. He had fallen behind his men while discussing efforts with the medics, along with his favorite fellow in the platoon. Cliff Crassus was the smallest man there, but they were told he had given more than any man to get where he was. He simply said that he was still standing.

Henry Eubank had a strong neck and posture, black features, and large hands. He was smarter than everyone else, they were not just saying it, and I think he had a fear of me. Mckenzie would catch him staring at Lee, who often fiddled with his bulletproof Bible at night. I think this made him the smartest man of all. I liked to watch him the most because he was a curiosity to Mckenzie and myself. I would look at him and study his movements. I would try and see what made him different and why he was still alive.

His back was a geographical map of scar tissue and tension. He slept awfully and then well; most days he woke with a crick. He enjoyed counting. He would count the men belonging to him in his platoon. He started this habit early on, and by the second day of June, he was counting ten less men and the remaining were unfamiliar bodies. He never tuned anyone or anything out, and for this, Mckenzie began to believe that John hated him. John was trying his very best not to listen to the lists of casualties every day. And when Mackenzie created this theory, he could not get rid of the image in his head, John with full hair and cheekbones leaning over a bus seat to peer at a younger man.

Henry was handsome. He wasn't white. Mckenzie began to realize that the other men disliked him. He came upon this realization when he first heard an irritable soldier telling the "Red Skin" to get him some real fucking water. Mckenzie shared the same water plea. He liked Henry. Henry was straightforward and described death as how it was. Maybe that was why he was disliked; he didn't seem to fear the inevitable future of violence.

Cliff Crassus was twenty, a year younger than Major Eubank. His breath, miraculously, always smelled of minty cough drops and pharmaceutical herbs. He was as experienced as the Major and had been with him for as long as he chose to remember. The innocence was retained in his youthful gloom. He was brown-eyed, the short claw of hair on his head the same shade, hair that Mckenzie would describe as completely unexceptional. His height was perhaps the one trait that was not entirely respected, but his limbs were thick enough to create a welt on your back with a tap. He shot accurately and never bit at his fingernails. Over mealtimes, he spoke at length on what he called the pillagers, the barbarians, the rapists, and what they thought of their mongrel nation. The Yamatos believed the American Navy to be a personal country club of golfers and bridge players. He metaphorically, somehow, called himself a weak-willed sybarite. Mckenzie didn't like him much. He once told Mckenzie, as a Japanese soldier was approaching, that he felt a sick sort of exhilaration when he hit one. Mckenzie would kill one just then, and he would never forget those words.

The afternoons of their jobs were not envious. Eubank spent his time observing the injured and studying their wounds, reflecting on the damage and telling the patient the truth directly; Cliff Crassus would go off and tell the medic if there was work to be done on the man or not. Their makeshift hospital areas were better than the enemy's, and this they reveled in. Henry Eubank wanted to be a doctor back home. Cliff was the one who told the medics to move on when they reached Jack Betchel. By nightfall, they were helping distribute meals, their tin cans of C-Ration, and the stuff from Guadalcanal. They tried their hardest not to roll their eyes at the disastrous liquids. They filled each canteen with the water, the kind taken from the uncleaned oil barrels, and took their own sips last. In the middle of the night, they woke with lizard skin for lips and throats. They rubbed mud onto their sores and sighed as it cooled their burns. But after a few seconds of relief, it heated up and irritated itself into further infection. The bedding problem did not help this. The two merely traded their dryer sheets in exchange for soaked ones. That night, they would watch a young recruit sleep a little sounder.

Mckenzie encountered truly lying flat on the ground for the first time. The company had been lucky; the sky dried up briefly and they had made it to a large patch of land closer to the beach than they had been before. At the sight of such ground, Al collapsed with sheer delight and giggled, the wet sand a disarray in his curls of the same color. Mckenzie clutched at John and Lee's elbows and dragged them to sit down. And they were all sitting with the ocean as their music, waiting for the enemy that sat in their own lines. Mckenzie took a deep breath, letting the salt flavor linger in his chest before pushing it out. He felt heady with enjoyment.

"Do you think the tide is going out?" said Cliff Crassus. Mckenzie did not know him. He was looking at the Major whose people called Red Skin.

"Maybe it's coming in," said Vicky.

"It's not," Henry Eubank said, but not rudely. "It's going out. Keep your hand on your rifle."

Sammy Brenner leaned into view. "What are you doing, Rye?"

Mckenzie started. He had been staring at the small gap in the forest that previewed the sky, right above John's head. "I'm thinking about things," he said.

John looked at him.

Mckenzie looked away.

He really was thinking about things. He was thinking about how some Sunday mornings, his parents would drive him to the beach. And they would sit together and he would terrorize beach ants and kick sand at seagulls. And the sun was always out just the right amount, so their skin had a healthy glow when looking in the back of a spoon, and the sky was bluer than depression dreams. He must have been barely nine.

In Okinawa, the sky was muggy and colorless, regardless of blue or black, and it felt damp without a break. Okinawa air was a smoker's exhalation.

"Have you guys been across the sea?" asked Cliff. Mckenzie realized with a jolt that he was talking to *their* group.

"No," said Stroshine. "We've been here shortly, I'd say."

"Two weeks or more."

"The weather is awful," said Cliff.

"We spent a spell in Iwo Jima," said Henry. He cleverly rolled a cigarette from a dried leaf.

Mckenzie held out a lit match for him.

Henry focused his attention on him and looked him intently in the face. "Thank you." He breathed the smoke up into the sky so it would not burn anyone's eyes. Mckenzie specifically remembered thinking how noble he believed this to be.

They ate their scarce lunches and walked onto the empty stretch of beach. He restrained himself from sprinting his weak legs through the sand and plowing into the water. He took in the salt again and would later taste it in his dreams. They dug for their positions and they waited. They did not wait long.

Mckenzie saw a vision of apprehension coming into his eye range and he knew then that they were coming and he would not have to deal with such feelings for long. Soon he would shoot and there would be nothing but straight firing and the forgiveness of muscle memory from a man older than he, one who was experienced simply in age, and on his deathbed, found he could not forget the faces behind the bullet.

There was that thump in his chest, and he felt at his heart through his Army-issued jacket. He wiped the sweat off of his brow.

Strange language. Strange noise. It was becoming more familiar with every day and every hour and minute and second. He bet that he would be able to translate Japanese fluently when this was over, and he had that thought as he began to shoot, aiming for torsos and watching them fall, his imagination cutting the heads off of them so they were wandering without a last wish.

He could have closed his eyes and continued to press down, lying flat in the sand on his stomach, and hear the voice of Travers screaming at Stroshine behind him. He could have felt at home like this.

There were more of them coming and he kept up at it. He could not fathom how one beach could house so many of them he could not count. Beside him on the right, lying on the ground as well, was Henry Eubank, who *was* counting. On Mckenzie's left was Cliff Crassus.

The number of men was dwindling, and out of the corner of his eye, he saw that John was still propped up. The relief was overwhelming.

One Jap was still approaching. He was stumbling. He would not make it far without falling. Perhaps he had been shot in both knees. But he was still advancing. Mckenzie raised his gun a little subconsciously. And everything began to move slower.

Cliff Crassus spoke next to him, and at the time, Mckenzie couldn't decipher if he was meant to be the listener.

"I feel some sort of sick exhilaration when I shoot one," he said. "Raise your gun a little."

Mckenzie did.

"Shoot, shoot," Cliff sighed and leaned closer, mumbling to himself.

Mckenzie did.

It was a headshot. The first of his life.

Kanto, a boy named after an earthquake that hit the Kanto Region of Japan, named by his scar-borne mother, fell to the sand and died as quickly as he lived.

33.

He was shaken awake.

"Micky," John was whispering in his ear, his breath hot and frantic. "Micky, I see something out there."

In an instant, Mckenzie sat up, fumbling with his gun, and looked to where John was pointing. His friend's drawn face, now pale from the lack of sunlight, was focused on a spot of motion several hundred meters to the left. Mckenzie pushed his back against the tree and grimaced slightly at the scrape of the bark against his spine, and he aimed as well as one could.

His vision finally adapted to the dark and what he was seeing. He *thought* he saw two figures twirling, dancing. They were spinning each other.

He froze.

"Do you see that?" John said, and his croaky voice made Mckenzie jump.

"What is that?" Mckenzie murmured. He let his fingers relax.

"There's a person down there, but I don't think it's a Jap," John whispered again.

"Well yeah, there's two of them."

John nudged his shoulder. "Two people? I just saw one."

"No, no. There's two. They're dancing."

"What the hell are you talking about? I don't see that."

Mckenzie pulled John into a similar position facing the people, wincing at the loud movement, and pointed with his free hand.

"Look. Two people. They're dancing."

John creased his eyebrows and shook his head. "I don't see it. I just see one person."

"How? Actually look, are you even looking?"

"Yeah, yeah, I'm looking." John frowned, then dove for his bag and took out his flashlight. Looking carefully around at the other men, making sure most were still asleep, he flicked it on and pointed it at the people.

The clearing was empty.

John and Mckenzie stared at it for a moment before John turned the flashlight off.

Mckenzie gave a shaky sigh, and his head fell back against the rough tree bark. He could see the Okinawa sky perfectly from this angle, although he figured it was the same sky everywhere. The stars were out.

"The stars are out tonight," he said.

"There's nobody out there," John said. He copied Mckenzie's stance and relaxed against the tree trunk. "It's just the weird shadows and the wind."

Mckenzie looked over at John. He was watching Lee, who was sleeping a few feet away, his blonde hair perfectly touched and his hands supporting his head. John looked back. He tilted his chin down, and the remaining moonlight lingered on the bridge of his nose and the concaves around his eyes, the dried mud on his neck the details of a painting. Mckenzie on instinct waved his hand over John's nose and mouth. He was still breathing

He was sure suddenly that John was empty inside.

Suddenly John was a doctor and Mckenzie the patient; suddenly John seemed as though he was examining someone for whom he had no particular thoughts for. He was acting how he had when Jack Betchel had finally died, and for a brief moment, Mckenzie wished for the John who became tearful when mad men were taken away.

He felt guilty all the time now.

"I'm going to sleep," John breathed, and sitting exactly as he was, he let his eyes fall shut. A small blip of comfort rose in Mckenzie in the fact that John did not move away from him. He just looked so strangely comfortable sleeping in nature that Mckenzie wondered if sleep was John's only redemption from humanity. He wasn't moving away, his healthy, paced breath hitting Mckenzie, and the feeling was a comfort, so that when he looked at John, he never had the stupid, wild fear that maybe his friend was dead. He was alive and right there was the proof.

I've heard that the method of nature is something to be wary of. The old tale goes that we feed the ones above us and are fed by the ones below, and so on. Our earth was made to be a futile system. It replenishes itself when everything has run out, until slowly, we are only what has created us. Mckenzie thought about this for a moment, and he thought that someday they would all be nothing but growth in the ground, and him too. This thought didn't hurt him much anymore.

He closed his eyes and focused on John's breathing.

And Mckenzie thought, *I promise I will never die in front of him.*

34.

He dropped onto the grass, calloused hands clutching at the earth, and he counted them as Henry Eubank did, counted each finger and then each knuckle, one by one, until he was counting out loud and Lee was hitting him around the head.

"Stand up," he said.

He did not stand up.

Instead, Mckenzie pressed his smudged face into his hands and tugged at his eyes.

—

There were no supplies. Meaning zero. Or very, very close to zero. They had been dwindling from the war effort, and few supplies even made it to the shore, while an injury ensured a lift home and a life, if you were not seriously injured. Unless you forwent help.

Mckenzie hated that. He hated that they had to pile mud onto Betchel's body with their entrenching tools, until he succumbed to the elements or somebody picked him up and brought him out. He hated the sleeping tactics of the Japs, how they'd wait until nightfall to gather in their little infiltrating groups, and send down their artillery and mortar fire until the enemy was trapped beneath the shadows of the rolling hills, the beautiful stretches of field. They crouched behind stone walls and lurked in the bare rice paddies with their caked layer of dust and fermenting human remains. Joe Marshall was always vomiting, and now his wrist was but the width of a bottle's neck. The scent was no longer pine trees, or maybe it was, somewhere where he was not, but Mckenzie was continuously submerged in a bath of damp fragrance, one that spun particles of crushed larvae and soil down into his lungs. He breathed in the expired air day in and day out. He slapped maggots off their cartridges in the rain. But at least they were not in mud.

Before they retired to closing one eye at night, Cliff Crassus would tell them stories of his previous fights. He and Eubank had seen far more than Mckenzie, and whenever they talked of it, he dug deeper into the soles of his boots, melting in overwhelming guilt. He ignored this as best as possible. The feeling returned, however, when Cliff told the tale of a fifteen-year-old Marine who had lied to his eager enlisting sergeant, and stumbled upon their company with his own all dead. They had the boy airlifted off to Guam, arguing that he could not be much use anyhow besides his age, when he was completely and forever in shock.

John entertained his friends the best he could, and when he no longer could, when every one of his memories had been buried in the explosions, Mckenzie took over. He happened to have something the others did not; he had spent the years previous to '45 living out his teenage life, and they had sat nervously around a radio and refused to meet the enlistees when they wished to say goodbye. So he told them about his life without the war in it, when he didn't know their names. Mostly, he told them about himself and Telly and how they painted ugly portraits of each other on their free afternoons, and how childish yet genius his tutor was. He laughed to himself, thinking of the day when Telly had arrived at his house to find Mckenzie holding unblown balloons, full tubes of acrylic paint, and darts. His parents were livid to find the paint splattered on the floor, most of it never reaching the canvas, and to find that Telly had mysteriously disappeared before they could lecture him. They had pushed each other around and pissed each other off, and finally, their last parting was an argument and a final reassurance. It was typical for their relationship.

Sometimes, Mckenzie would look over at John and marvel at his annoyed expression, for he had not seen it in a fortnight. John didn't have emotions anymore. Most of the time, he sat and did his work and shot and killed and lived. But whenever Mckenzie began these stories, John became irritated. The others just looked sad. And he hated him, he hated John for being so weak, for his thinning skin and limbs, how little he did *anything.* Mckenzie never knew it was possible to hate something no longer human. He was no longer physical.

Mckenzie finished his talking for the night. He did not miss the way the other recruits looked longingly at him, and he knew that they were thinking that if they were in his place, they never would have come here. John was frowning, of course. Mckenzie felt a surge of anger. John was never happy, and although none of them could be, why couldn't he just be normal for once?

"What's wrong now?" he asked John as the others were settling their bedding.

"Nothing," he said, and, of course, it wasn't nothing. It was always something.

"No, what is it?"

John rubbed at his eyes hard enough to paint the whites pink. "I'm sorry I'm always hitting you."

Mckenzie stared at him, confused. "What do you mean?"

"I'm sorry I hit you."

"Yeah. You hit me once. When we were on our way here."

"I'm sorry about that."

"But…" Mckenzie shook his head. "You said that you're sorry you're *always* hitting me. You only hit me once."

John rolled over on his bedding so that he was no longer facing Mckenzie. He was far away when he said, "I feel like I'm always hitting you."

Mckenzie didn't know what to say to this.

John sprung back up suddenly and turned to Mckenzie with a strange vigor, his eyes wide and firm. "You know, I love Lee. He's my best friend. I met him in grade school. He's my brother."

"I know that."

"Can I explain something to you?"

He said yes.

"It's like," John fumbled for words. "It's like—I've seen you mad before. Not very, very mad, but I've seen you mad. And when you're angry, you get this feeling. And you have to get the feeling out. 'Cause you can't breathe with it."

Mckenzie listened to him.

"That's how I feel," John said. "I have to get the bad feelings out. When I do, I'll be myself again."

35.

Their house had been packed up for a while; steadily over time, so Telly had not noticed. He thought perhaps he had not seen it before because he, of course, was too immersed in his own troubles. He met his best friends on their driveway, the moving trucks filled up, and he saw the FOR SALE sign for the first time, and saw that it was being taken down.

Some lucky bastard bought the house, Telly thought. And now they would get a life without care. It probably had gone off the market in seconds. Living spaces in town, no matter the cost or condition, were sold quickly, probably because the cost for the house was less than the cost outside, the cost that could be your life.

Carrie and Rico were hauling boxes out to the movers, only a few stray ones remaining on their doorstep. Rico stumbled and dropped his box directly on his foot; he yelped over the clatter of a lamp hitting the pavement. Carrie, used to his years of clumsiness, ignored him and continued walking to the moving truck.

"I swear," gasped Rico upon seeing Telly. "I swear, I've always hated that stupid lamp."

Telly waved off his advancements. "I just came to say goodbye," he said.

At twenty-six, he was remembering how incredibly excited he was when his best friend began to settle down and have children. He remembered very clearly the heroics of their first day together, how he soared into a battle between four (or had it been three) brats, the littlest being smacked around until his rescue, and the short thanks that was not really a thank you at all, a friendship that lasted seventeen years, living close by, visiting, lunch with his wife, watching his kids. And now there was this separate future, one with a draft and panic, newspapers with actual news and dead-boy eulogies and happy times, too. They would celebrate Christmas and toast Harry, as Carrie always called him, lick their dinner plates clean, go off to work and hire a sitter, sit by the fire and talk. He reconciled with the fact that seventeen years could not beat the rest of their lives without him. They would go on without living parallel, and one day, he would be called to speak about their best moments, and he would see every single second of it alone.

"Well, then. Help me with the box," Rico said.

"I like to watch you struggle. Go get your kid to do it."

"Telly." They turned around to see Carrie empty-handed. "He's slacking."

"Yeah, he's a loser."

—

The three of them shoved the remaining boxes into the rented moving truck. They kept their talking light. They talked about the weather and work and reprimanded Frank, in the case of Rico, after seeing his son giddily push their boxes out of the van. Telly studied Carrie. Her blonde hair was pulled back, her freckled youthful face residing in her children, her posture firm yet comfortable. She was confident in her every belief and decision, and this one was no different. He had never envied another person as he did her.

The final box was packed away, and they looked at each other with sighs of relief in the sweet summer afternoon, and an empty house stood behind them. Telly knew that his friends were concerned for the kids; Donna and Ines were too young to have made many attachments, but the town was the only home Frank had ever known. He'd be fine, thought Telly. He was *excited* to leave, and Telly didn't know if that was a problem or not.

He found his godson crouching among the hazy azaleas, poking at the dirt. He had started gelling his hair back like his father; it was wispy pieces that were a color much lighter than the Italian's. He had his mother's face. Telly wondered if he would inherit her attitude, and Rico's humor, and he hoped for it.

"Hey, little man," said Telly. Frank looked up at him.

"You lied," he said, grinning. "You said you knew Mr. Bartholdi and you don't 'cause he's been dead a million years."

"Mr. Bartholdi?" Then Telly remembered. "Frédéric Auguste Bartholdi?"

"The Mister who did the Statue of Liberty!"

"Yeah. That's him. No, I guess I don't know him. I got him mixed up with another Frédéric Auguste Bartholdi."

"There's another one?"

"Yep," said Telly. "Do you know that the Statue of Liberty—well, it's called Liberty Enlightening the World?"

"No, I sure didn't."

"Pretty funny name. That's why we gave it a nice nickname."

"What's liberty?" Frank asked, mulling over the syllables.

Telly sighed and thought. "Well, I guess it's freedom. So being able to do whatever you wish, or choosing not to eat vegetables."

"I like vegetables."

"Yuck. I didn't when I was your age. I applaud you, youngster."

"What's enlightening?"

"Turning on a light," said Telly.

"No kidding," said Frank, giggling and crouching further into the flowers. "I do that all the time."

"Then you are what they call an enlightener."

"That's cool," Frank said. "Will there be other enlighteners in Philadelphia?"

Telly had almost forgotten that.

"Yeah, they have them everywhere."

"Good. I don't want to be around people who don't turn lights on."

"That would mean they are very stupid, if they don't turn lights on."

"I think so, too," said Frank.

Carrie and Rico's entire house was packed away, and there was no longer a need to linger, but Frank was whining. Besides, Telly told them he had a surprise. He had a going-away gift, if you will.

The family and Telly drove to his house and left the moving truck in the driveway. They entered his living room, the little ones abuzz, and Frank clapped with delight.

"What's that?" he said, bouncing on his toes.

Telly had set up a large blank canvas. Taped to it were several full balloons.

"Balloons. You fill them with paint, and tape them to the canvas and throw darts at them," he said.

"Do you have darts?" Donna leaped with excitement.

"We could use knives," said Telly.

"Oh my gosh." Carrie's eyes widened. "You've lost it. Rico, he's lost it. He's giving the kids knives."

Telly laughed. "No, no. I have darts. Go on and try it."

Rico, in his usual childish fashion, went first. He threw the dart and it dropped without popping a balloon.

"Okay, I wanna go, 'cause Dad is bad at it!" cried Frank. He took a dart from Telly, turned back to him and said his thank you, and threw it. It popped one balloon and red paint splattered a section of the canvas. It just barely dusted the hardwood floors.

"You should stay for dinner," said Telly. He, Rico, and Carrie were content in watching the kids throwing darts giddy with joy at the mess they were making.

"I wanna stay for dinner!" Donna garbled and knocked her little sister Ines in the head gently. Ines sniffed.

"I'll let you guys stay for dinner," said Telly. "But not your mom and dad. I heard recently that they don't approve of my methods."

36.

There was a man being lifted onto dry ground horizontally. The day's brief recess was over with the coming rain of shells; they crouched together in their fox holes and asked for no harm. In the morning, they dusted themselves off, pulled the others to their feet, and were left with an ally wounded in Mckenzie's range.

He was blonde-haired and the perfect model for some Aryan aggression if this was another land. Bits of shrapnel? had clamped to his knee, and while he would not die from the wound, he would not be able to walk. At this point, Mckenzie thought, that man would be able to go home with that injury. Mckenzie almost longed to shoot himself, and yet there was still a fear of pain. A fear that he would be caught or would accidentally die when it was not intended. Instead of putting his gun to his stomach, he watched the others heave the injured man onto steady ground. Behind him, Marshall and Brenner were discussing the German Mauser K98.

"It's not too painful," said the injured man. "I'd have thought it would be worse." He fixed his large, kind eyes on his beholders. Then he looked up.

"You can see the Pleiadian constellation from here," he said.

John made a noise. Mckenzie whipped his head around, and saw that he was laughing, throwing his head back with genuine emotion. He was feeling *something*, and whether that feeling counted as hysteria or not, Mckenzie didn't care. John was feeling something, and something was better than nothing.

Mckenzie looked up. The funny thing, he supposed, was that if there was a constellation that could be seen from Okinawa, they were not seeing it. Although it was morning, the sky had darkened at the edges like a burnt piece of their tin meals until it was completely, life-haltingly dark, and the light rain, lighter than it had been in days, was coming down in a vision of mystery. But he knew that phrase from somewhere. He felt as though he had heard it long ago.

"Hey," he was saying without his own knowledge. He came closer to the injured man, who was smiling with the rain hitting his face as if he was sunbathing. The man smiled benignly.

"What's your name?" asked Mckenzie.

"You know him?" Dorman said lazily, itching at his leg through his boot.

"Major Lewis Gagney," he said. "From North Dakota."

"You know him?" said Dorman.

"No. I don't know that name, sorry. You just looked familiar."

"Well, come here," said Lewis Gagney. "Let me see you."

Mckenzie hovered over the man and leaned a bit closer, so that he could see his face.

Lewis pointed at him as he lay flat on his back, relaxed, his right knee charred with blood and small chunks of hot metal that once had been flying through the trees.

"You can see the Pleiadian constellation from here," Lewis Gagney said.

He's gone insane, thought Mckenzie. And then he remembered.

"I do know you. I recognize you from somewhere," Lewis said before Mckenzie could form any words.

"Yeah, yeah. I met you on the ships."

"What ships?"

"The transport ships. Fleets."

"Ah."

"I recognized you," Mckenzie continued. "When you said that thing about the Pleiadian constellation. You were talking about that when I met you."

"I paint it sometimes."

"Yes, yes. That's how I know you. I saw you, you know, in the sleeping barracks, and you were painting, and you said you'd smuggled in painting supplies, and you were painting the Pleiadian constellations. You let me have a look."

"Did I?" He did not sound surprised.

"Yes."

"What did you think of it? My work?" asked Lewis.

Mckenzie frowned and didn't quite know what to say.

"I've painted some beautiful things before," Lewis said when he didn't answer, "or I've modeled my paintings off of beautiful things, and I must say, it really makes me want to kill myself."

Mckenzie did not want to ask why he felt so, but he did anyhow.

"Beautiful things cause me so much pain. Much more than the pain that is in this wound of mine."

"He's crazy," murmured John behind Mckenzie, who was slightly shocked at his presence. He turned around in childish fright and stared at the two of them, two men he was beginning to view as outlandish, wearily.

"You're going home, Major," said Dorman. "It's your lucky day."

"It's always a lucky day when a man has shrapnel in his knee."

This time, Lee snorted. Vicky Halsted, who was examining a deep cut on his cheekbone with interest, smiled as well. Most of the men around him, wiping absently at their own dirt-stained faces, were eating out of their cans, their tongues dry. Some of them were watching Lewis Gagney and his captivating way of entertaining. Well, it *was* entertainment after all.

"You're crazy," said John, smiling. He was really smiling. The sight made Mckenzie smile.

"Crazy, that is just an opinion. You know what's crazy?" Lewis said loudly, wincing through the medic examining his wound. "I've got metal in my knee. What's a man supposed to do without a knee? May as well have it up my ass, too."

John was really laughing now. The silent shaking, bent over shoulders laughing, and Lee was doing it, too.

"Are assholes really that important, or have we just assumed that they are?" said a passing White.

"Yes, they are extremely important!" said Lewis. "Without an ass, you might retract into your own body from all the shit."

"You're crazy," said John. "Medic, please, fix this man up a drink."

"He's acting like he's already had several," said the medic, and John howled.

By late afternoon, Lewis Gagney had been taken off the beaches to get his knee sewed back up. Sergeant Travers was standing nearby. He came closer to Mckenzie, observing as the others watched Lewis being hoisted up into the supply jeep, which would take him to the village. He was silent as the vehicle drove off. His blue eyes were as foggy as they had been when they were first introduced. He had a bit of a gash under his eye, but he was alright. He was twenty-eight.

"That fellow has been right behind me this whole time," he said.

Mckenzie frowned at him.

"While we've been going wherever we are going, while we ate and slept, that fellow was right near me. And he was talking the whole time," Travers said.

Mckenzie cleared his throat before speaking. "About what?"

"He was saying that if he ever got injured, he wouldn't aim to live. He said that he would aim to make it funny."

Travers nodded politely to him and waited for a nod back. When he got it, he walked leisurely toward the front of the group. He was whistling. When Mckenzie turned back around, he was met with John. He was nodding too, and lighting one of his last cigarettes. When the fire flickered like film over his eyes, Mckenzie could see every different shade of brown. He wanted to paint them. He was afraid that one day, that brown would be like every other shade.

There were breaks in every piece of humanity. I saw them all. I witnessed every remainder of these wrecks. They lived on and no one remembered them. They spent their time in the pews and talked to me as well as they knew how. Some of them wrote it down and some of them were diagnosed. Others found that they could no longer see angels or play with their babies. They could no longer cry over dead dogs.

37.

June 16th. One a.m.

There was a resounding bang overhead; nothing new, the same sound he heard as he slept. But this one, Mckenzie felt, was different.

He was strangely used to the sounds of fighter planes colliding at night, the clashing, the hot metal searing gashes into the gaping, wet earth, each impact like a deathmatch in his ear canal. Every night was one long hour of shaking smaller recruits in the lull of sleep, and stumbling upon a form that had not been moving for a while. They counted their fingers, and when a certain shell was dropped one night, Stroshine was counting one less.

Mckenzie sat up. He had pushed his bedroll to the side before going to sleep, and now he was slowly freezing where he sat, although the weather had been stifling that day. His legs were cramping, bent against the cold sand, and the sneaking tendrils of beach grass curled around his knees, and his back was pressed against a rocky ridge of assorted plants, the kinds he could not tell the difference between. The island was always giving the air of being a secretive hiding spot, but no place as much as the beaches, Mckenzie thought. The jungle had been an open hell, the fields were irritating, but the beaches held a wild beauty that could trick a man into eating a poisonous flower. He detested them. But still, he held place in the crashing of the waves on the shoreline, continuous and never stopping. It was the only sound he could rely on, besides the planes and the shelling. But Mckenzie knew, this time, the sound was different.

He crawled over the piled-up men, careful not to wake them, across the sand, to where the quiet sea slept. It brushed the shore like a hair comb. Sitting on his knees, his pant legs deep in the wet ground, he cupped the salt water in his closed palms. He brought it to his mouth. He let the burning bubbles touch his skin, and he let it spill out from between his fingers, the mixture of life-in-death slipping away from him once more. He's becoming something else, something inhuman. Human beings drank regular water and lived in peace, whether in civilization or not. Now he was beyond human, beyond present time. He had become the kind of cautionary tale that has been told since the beginning of time; *don't try to be a hero*. And he lived in the in-between, where loved ones write the undying letters. He lived in the death in life, and the life in death.

What the *hell* was he doing here?

Even beyond humanity, he was human and he was thirsty.

John was awake holding his rifle to his chest when Mckenzie returned from the water. He was wide-eyed. Mckenzie understood then that John understood him; he understood more in the world than the highest power, and he would see to the end with a kind of forgiveness that the world was empty of. John was hearing the same sound, and he was distinguishing the differences between the last few nights, how they had been lying in wait for some time now, how they couldn't wait forever for the enemy to make themselves known if steadily the days were running out, the calendar turning too fast for a human to glimpse, and now it was one in the morning. It was one in the morning, and John was awake, and he and Mckenzie were hearing something strange as the others slept, and as surely as they knew the Japs were losing and would not give up, they knew this: something was coming.

"Get the others up," John said. He didn't bother to whisper; the enemy couldn't hear him anyhow, but the men were always whispering, whispering or screaming.

Mckenzie did. He roused the others in his vicinity as quickly as possible, and John was assembling his gear. He was assembling his gear and his eyes were dry and his hands were not shaking, but Mckenzie's were. Mckenzie tapped Lee's shoulder, watching as down the line of troops, one by one, the men began to wake up from that sense of urgency in the air.

Lee didn't say anything. He took in the expression lit on Mckenzie's pale face, the brightest splotch of color in the moody night and he knew.

"What did you see?" Lee said.

Mckenzie was unable to tell him. He was unable to point out the sound he was hearing. He began to question if it was real.

"I hear it," said Sammy Brenner. He was frantically packing up his things, rolling up his bed, dusting the sand off. "I hear that, too. Where's Travers?"

Joe Marshall was rubbing his eyes drowsily beside William White and Mike Stroshine, both looking as though they had swallowed a difficult pill. Sid Dorman helped Sammy Brenner pack his gear and then stood up and set to waking others. Al and Vicky Halsted were kneeling close together, their elbows touching, and they looked so exactly alike that it was frightening. Kenny Greene was already standing, ready to move, and Mckenzie stared at him and wondered if he was ever sleeping.

Travers was talking to Henry Eubank and Cliff Crassus. He had his hands folded against his abdomen. Cliff was pacing. Henry was nodding. All around them, the sea of men was awakening and they were readying themselves and muttering. They spoke a chorus of similar words and I caught every one. I felt the heaviness wash over myself.

Mckenzie stood up slowly. He heard it easily now, the footsteps, the rustling in the forest behind them—

He realized.

It occurred to him, just then, that it wasn't what he was hearing that scared him. It was what he wasn't hearing.

For the first time in his memory, maybe the first time he had stepped foot on the island, the explosions of colliding planes and bombs and shells had stopped, and Okinawa was completely silent.

He killed more than a few men since the start of June, and now he was beginning to understand that all those deaths were bringing him to the death of something bigger. He saw victory so clearly now. It was there, right in front of him, and he understood, he knew the enemy would do anything to push it away.

Then somebody screamed.

It was as if the ground suddenly reverberated and lifted them up into the sky in one burst of lightning. He was feeling nothing at all, until the impact was on every one of his bones, and they were slick with rain, of course because it never stopped raining—

Was he sitting or standing? Was he laying on the sand? Was he injured or just dead? It was only the impact ringing in his ears, the rush of incoming men and shooting. Guns. He was seeing every color imaginable, and in that, he was seeing his entire life flashing before his eyes.

In the bright explosions of light, hurtful in the dark, Mckenzie was pulling the trigger countless times. He was taking head shots and running and falling and crouching. He was being dragged. His vision came back for a split second; he saw John hiding beside him, the terror so plain on his face Mckenzie was sure he was sick. He was vomiting.

He was running then, John pulling him by the hand, his feet almost flying with the speed they were moving, kicking up sand and warm, white bubbling water.

He was not dead.

He saw one man fall in a painful way. It was a Japanese man. Mckenzie was the one to shoot him.

How long did it go on for? It was like he had a heat stroke. He was stumbling, the edges of his vision blurring together, his muscles moving from pure adrenaline—

In the next moment, everything changed.

Mckenzie was running behind John. He aimed his rifle. He shot. When he looked to his right, he could just see the stars in the sky, the ocean, and three lone Jap soldiers. They were hovering close to the edge of the rocky hills. They were huddling together, pointing their guns at the two men by their feet, unarmed in American greens. Mckenzie briefly saw one of the Americans swing his fist at the Jap's muzzle; they swatted him and shot him. Mckenzie saw a flash of blonde hair and blood go down. Not Lee, his mind comprehended fast enough. Sammy Brenner. His thinking was one mantra: take them out, be the offensive. The other

American, the living one, was being pulled up. He was being held by the three Japanese.

Mckenzie was so confused.

The three Jap soldiers were dragging the American into the forest urgently, and in seconds they were gone.

And Mckenzie was sprinting into the forest in another direction, stumbling among the roots with his fellow footmen, and the Japs were retreating, the fire was ceasing to a stop, he was collapsing on the ground, his eyes blurry with sweat or blood, his entire body burning, and Lee Collins was taken deeper into the island, feeling the rope blindly as he went, a prisoner completely alone.

38.

June 15th. One a.m. America.

Telly opened his eyes in the heavy dark. He had heeded Carrie's advice and begun to take advantage of the heating in his house. He nudged the sheets gently off his arms. The alarm clock on his bedside table read one a.m. clearly. He felt a little spooked at waking at such an exact time. The feeling went away.

He was looking at June. She was sleeping, wrapped up like a child in his blankets, in his bed. He wasn't even mad that she had stolen all of them and he had woken with half a sheet on his torso. He smiled. Is this what love was? Letting somebody steal the sheets at night? Because he did love her, if that was possible. He had never known another person to be so present as she always was. But he was overthinking it now. Maybe he simply felt a strong tie of endearment toward her.

Telly had once heard a saying from his mother and father. They were drinking wine and discussing something. He had interrupted them. It was late in the night and he had had a terrible nightmare and did not expect to find them awake.

"You know, darling," his mother said, "if you wake up in the hours one to four in the night, that is God trying to tell you something. He's trying to talk to you."

Telly thought of this now. What was God trying to tell him?

He smiled at sleeping June. I know her, he thought. I know her and she knows me better than she knows herself. We are each other's people. She's my people. And I think God is trying to tell me that. He is telling me to not fuck it up. He is telling me that what I have waited for is coming and it will get here faster with *her*, because she is it. I feel that and God feels it, He must. He ignored the last flash inside of him, the last nagging question before the morning came, when he would know the answer. Let me have this one moment. Let me have clarity; let it all come loose.

Telly cautiously rolled over in bed, facing June. She was breathing evenly with her plain brown hair parted and tucked tight behind her ears. Her nose was bunched up and pressed into the pillows.

He thought, I'd let you have every pillow I've got, if it meant this. He let sleep enchant him back under. He fell asleep to thoughts of her.

And here, I had woken him up, and found I didn't know how to tell him.

39.

June 16th. Six a.m.

Sammy Brenner was a tough loss, Travers contended. Their company was scattered around an acre of forest, and Travers was speaking to his men from basic training, all of them in a circle. Sammy Brenners was a tough loss. He had an excellent sharp eye.

And Lee, thought Mckenzie. *Don't forget about Lee.* He watched an ant crawled across the toe of his boot. The blood on his hands was no longer art; it was something that no matter any number of years or damage, it would return, unscathed, to cover the next men to come along.

"And Collins," Travers added, meeting Mckenzie's eye. He must have spoken aloud.

It was strange. He was safe, yet his whole being was shaking.

The remaining bodies on the land were Japanese. Most of the Americans had survived. There were varying scales of injuries down the line. Sammy Brenner was one of the biggest losses. But they had succeeded in forcing the enemy back a little bit further. The whole island would soon be theirs. There was no optimism to this way of thinking; it simply was fact.

"How do we know Collins didn't just take off?" Al leaned forward, shaking his head, and lit a cigarette. His face was bloody, especially above his eyebrow.

"He didn't. I saw them capture him. He's not a deserter," said Mckenzie with monotony.

"And if you're just saying that 'cause you know he'll be thrown in the pound if we ever get him back?"

"Hey," said John. For once, he was steady and composed. Stronger than he had been in weeks. "Hey. Lee is no deserter. Didn't you listen to Mckenzie? He saw the Japs nab him. You." He pointed at Travers. "You need to send a man from the company out to retrieve him. Lee's one of your best."

With zero emotion, Travers replied, "I don't take your orders."

John moved closer to him. He was firm in his words. "Then send me out. I can find him and bring him back without compromising our position."

Travers ignored him. Mckenzie was afraid. He was afraid of who was behind the trees; he was afraid of the man in the open.

"Look," said John. "You have a daughter? Her name's Leanna, you call her Lee? I remember that. I remember that from the first day. Don't you know that?"

There was a faint crack in the man, in those blue ocean eyes, where the emotion was stirring and where his whistling self had once been.

"I can find Lee. I can bring him back," John said. "I promise you. I won't be deserting my position. I won't ever do that. Rye says that only three Japs have got him. They couldn't have gotten far. You need to let me go."

"D'you ever think that Collins might already be dead?" Al said.

"Shut the fuck up," Mckenzie said. "Jesus fucking Christ." His throat ached and the instant fatigue he felt after yelling was a reward. The anger released toward Al was short-lived. There were always men yelling at each other, but none got as far as throwing punches, seeing as no one had the energy.

"Keep your head on," said Travers. Mckenzie glowered at the sergeant's reprimand.

"And St. Dennis," said Travers. He had recovered his cool demeanor, but Mckenzie had already noticed the slick, deep cuts on his temples. "You're not qualified for any of this. You probably never will be. If you were under some other sergeant, he might let you go off and kill yourself. I'm telling you now, the enemy doesn't go down easily. You think you're qualified for this, you're not."

"I know."

"You don't. You think you've seen it all, and you haven't. At this point, you've got to choose whose life you wanna save."

"Don't tell me how to live *my* life."

"I will if you want to get out of here. You want the rest of your short-lived life to be hell after hell? You want to be taken along with Collins? I strongly recommend you, boy, that you do this how I tell you."

"I'll do it my own way," said John. He stared Travers venomously and directly in the eye. "So go fuck yourself."

For once, Al Halsted was quiet. They were all silent. Dorman and Vicky were exchanging meaningful looks. White and Marshall nodded at John's words with expressions of something alike to pride. Stroshine was slumped, drifting between sleep and consciousness, against a tree. Greene kept his gaze on the dirt. Travers was going to hit him. He was going to hurt him. Why didn't he hit them? There was real fear in him now. It wasn't just the blood in his veins, it *was* his veins. He was made of it. Travers was such a *meek* man, so different from the other sorts of men that could have been in charge of them. *This changed nothing*, Mckenzie thought, in the end.

John would not change his decision. It had already been made. He was the kind of man where you could see his thoughts run out of his ears, and I knew then that this would be non-negotiable.

Mckenzie packed his gear as subtly as he could and gave a sweeping goodbye to the others in his head. For he knew John was leaving, and if John was leaving, so was he.

—

They would wait until the others were asleep before leaving. Mckenzie fell asleep in seconds, his arms wrapped around his head. When he woke, John was standing above him with his gear tucked into his shirt and swung over his shoulder. The group had settled down after the argument and gave up on debating who was the winner. Many of the men were taking a brief moment of sleep, which they did not get much of these days. Travers, miraculously, was nowhere near. It was far too easy. There were no irritated soldiers to stop them from leaving, no one to say that they were ruining the reputation of the company by leaving. Travers had said it was a death wish, and they were leaving, and somehow, they hadn't been threatened yet.

Too easy.

"I'm going now," John whispered. His face was cleaner than it had been in a while. "I'm going to get Lee, now."

"Okay, okay." Mckenzie groaned and pulled his things to his side, ignoring the eruption of fear in his heart. He strapped his pack on and stood up slowly, listening for the sound of his boots in the grass that could wake the others.

"I've got an idea of where they're going," said John quietly. "I've got some sense about it. I saw bits and pieces of what was going on, and I'll be alright."

"Yeah, we'll be fine. Maybe they won't notice we're gone," said Mckenzie. He sighed. That was stupid to say.

John furrowed his eyebrows at him.

"What?"

"No, never mind. Nothing," John said. "D'you think we're crazy for doing this?"

Mckenzie shrugged. "I haven't got any idea who's crazy and who's not anymore."

John nodded. "Yeah."

They took one last look at the remaining sleeping seven men. Mckenzie didn't know how he felt anymore.

"Hold up."

John and Mckenzie froze. This was the punchline when they hadn't even started the joke. They whirled around, expecting someone to slam them to the ground and shoot them, or arrest them.

Joe Marshall, his curly red hair matted, his dirt-stained cheekbones jutting out, was standing before them, his gear completely assembled for moving. He, unnoticeably, hadn't been sleeping. He was looking right at the two of them.

For some reason, the only thing Mckenzie's brain could conjure up was, Remember how he thought Harry Houdini was a mind reader?

John moved first. He leapt toward Marshall, both hands gripping his shoulder, and pulled him away from the sleepers. Then frantically he hissed, "Joe, you're not gonna say one *fucking* word about this. You're gonna go back to sleep and shut the fuck up. Got it?"

Mckenzie was still defrosting from his shock. "I don't know what you heard," he started.

"Jesus, I'm coming with you," Marshall whispered, his eyes narrowing as if to say, *the fuck did you think I was doing*? Like they should have known.

"What?"

"God, you too, huh?" John tugged hard at the skin under his eyes. "Are you fucking around or are you serious?"

"You know, I've known Lee just as long as you have," said Marshall. "I'm coming. I don't wanna stay here anyhow. Maybe some other company can pick us up once we have Lee."

Again, all Mckenzie's brain supplied him with was the memory of Marshall passed out in his barracks bed, John's pouting, determined lip, and the sudden realization that they shared days he would never be a part of. They had grown up together, and Mckenzie never really believed that until now. It was hard to picture the two men in a place other than war.

"Fine," said John, and Mckenzie almost began to argue for some unknown reason. "But we leave now."

"I'm ready," said Marshall.

John let a harsh breath out. "Okay. Let's go then."

John started walking north quickly, deeper into the forest, with Marshall following. Mckenzie looked back at the boys whom he had known since March. They were still sleeping. They seemed so young. There weren't any deeper things to say. To say that they were young was the most painful. It was the most truthful thing he could conjure up.

Mckenzie jogged to catch up to John and Joe. He fell into step beside them with a rapidly-beating heart. And so, the final journey began.

40.

June 16th. Seven a.m.

They had been walking for an hour. Or running. John had his compass out in his open palm; at random moments he would make a sharp turn in a new direction. He also had a map.

Mckenzie simply followed John and Joe into the forest. He no longer retained information. They were in the south, so they had to go north. They were Americans, so they killed Japs. They had one job: to push the Japanese together, to encircle and burn out another country, and he knew that they were winning, but winning wasn't supposed to feel like this.

The first ten minutes of walking led to an argument. John said that the Japs who captured Lee and killed Brenner had marched north into the woods, while Mckenzie maintained that they had taken off along the shoreline to the west. They fought for a few minutes about this, until Mckenzie realized that maybe he did see the Japs go into the forest. The three of them did agree that the Japs were possibly contemplating deserting, a rarity in their eyes, and stumbled upon Lee. Taking an American back would certainly increase their own chances of survival. John said that they couldn't have gotten far; their choices were leading John to believe that they were not the smartest of Imperial Japan. In hopes of finding Lee, Joe guessed that the Japs could have found a safe area for a rest nearby. They prayed for this to be true.

Mckenzie's lips were dry. He siphoned mud off his teeth and spat it out. Fatigue was returning in his bones, so that he began to marvel at how his brain could move each limb on command so easily. He let himself trust John and ignore his surroundings. He watched John and Joe interact for entertainment. He found it strange how Joe looked at John so differently from how Mckenzie himself looked at him. Then he remembered that John and Joe had entirely different memories together, and knowing someone in a different light would cause you to feel other emotions toward them. He realized that he and Joe would probably never treat John the same, or even think of him in the same way. Everything a person did was up for interpretation, and Mckenzie thought that you couldn't truly know a person unless you spent every single second with them.

—

It was, if his calculations were correct, eight p.m. on the fifteenth in America.

It was ten a.m, the sixteenth, in Okinawa. They were fourteen hours ahead.

He wondered what his parents were doing. Knowing them, they were probably ready for bed.

They had been walking north for three hours when John shushed them suddenly and dropped to the ground, laying on his stomach. Joe and Mckenzie followed. Through the gaps of twisted greenery, they could see a small clearing some meters away. In that clearing was a Japanese settlement fit for three men, three Japanese soldiers talking in a huddled group, and one American soldier, tied to a tree trunk with some kind of rope.

It was too easy.

Mckenzie's heart lurched with happiness, but beside him, John clenched his large jaw. Their legs were stretched back behind them, their bodies hidden fairly well in the tall grass and unknown plants. John propped his gun in front of him, keeping low, and aimed at the back of one Japs.

Wait, Mckenzie mouthed. *Wait.*

John let his finger linger on the trigger but did not pull.

The three Americans listened to the three Japanese.

John scooted forward on his elbows and raised his rifle once more. This time, Mckenzie did not object. He pulled his gun into place and pointed it at another man's head. Joe slowly dragged his through the grass and aimed.

A moment passed and the targets didn't move. So they pressed the triggers within seconds of each other.

Each of the Japanese soldiers stumbled forward with shocked yells, as though they had simply twisted an ankle. The blood spatter hitting the ground gave the illusion that they had all attacked one another; they were dropping, turning in shock, and their eyes were meeting Mckenzie's, and he raised his rifle in defense. One had crawled to his feet again, until a clean shot to his forehead ended him, and they were all dead. Mckenzie saw John, his eyes narrowed, finally releasing the trigger. All three Americans stood up and cautiously approached the enemy.

They were crumpled together, their limbs folded over each other, and it was a miracle that none of them were breathing. The shots had not been very precise. The blood ran fast from each wound. Their Army caps were drooping over their faces. Mckenzie was glad that he did not have to look them in the face.

John and Mckenzie were still looking at their kills when Joe sprinted over to the American soldier tied to the tree.

"Lee," said John.

They huddled around Lee. Joe feverishly, with shaking hands, untied the thick rope binding Lee to the base of the tree. His legs were splayed out, the knees of his Army-issued pants torn, and his mouth bloodied at the edges. His blonde hair, always neat without effort, was full of stray, dried bits of mud. His brown eyes were clear. And he wasn't saying anything.

"Don't talk," said John, although Lee was silent. His wrists were released, and they fell uselessly to his side, deep purple indentations from the fibers. "Drink that, c'mon, drink it." John forced his canteen to Lee's lips.

Lee swallowed one gulp, then pushed John's hand away.

"No, no. C'mon, drink some more." But Lee shook his head and pushed it away.

"Are hungry or something?" Mckenzie asked. He pulled an open lidded can out of his pack. "You want some, Lee?"

He shook his head. Joe brushed his clipped red hair out of habit and knelt closer to Lee. "D'they do anything to you?"

Lee sniffed and cleared his throat. "No, no. I'm fine. They just got me, that's all."

"Well, you're lucky they didn't get far, or we never would have found you," John said. He sighed and lay on his back, his spine pressed against the hard earth.

"Lucky they weren't the brightest group," said Joe.

"They weren't. They stopped for a rest about half an hour ago," said Lee. "And started arguing about me. I think that's what was going on. I figured they were all planning on deserting, and just wanted to bring back an American. Which is pretty rare."

Mckenzie was quiet. He watched Lee drink the rest of John's water. It was too easy. *Nothing* was ever this easy.

Lee coughed and gave John his canteen. "How are you here? Did you get some kind of leave or something to come and get me?"

Mckenzie, John, and Joe were silent.

"What?"

41.

June 16th. Twelve p.m.

Lee was swearing without taking a breath.

Lee never swears, Mckenzie thought.

"Are you out of your *fucking* minds?" Lee brought his shaking hands angrily to cover his face. "This is bad. Did you *think*—"

"Jesus, I told you. We were going to save your fucking ass. Now we did. And, oh look, we're fucking going back!"

"Maybe it won't matter in the long run," said Mckenzie. "I mean, we are going back. It's not like we were leaving the danger. It's not like we wasted time not killing Japs."

"*Maybe it won't matter*—oh my god. You fucking fools. You too, Micky."

"That's the first time you've ever called me 'Micky.'"

"Shut the fuck up."

Mckenzie smiled. His spirits had heightened considerably at finding Lee mostly unharmed besides a thin streak of resentment toward the three of them and a multitude of bruises already appearing on his arms. Now they walked back, dodging gnarled roots that twisted toward their ankles and sinisterly hissing trees. Maybe Mckenzie was villainizing the whole island. It was, truly, beautiful.

John and Joe both had out their compasses, Joe juggling his stained map as well. Mckenzie trusted the fact that they seemed to know where they were going. Meanwhile, he and Lee kept watch around them, Lee doing so in a much more paranoid fashion.

"You think we're almost back?" Joe asked.

"I bet so," John said knowledgeably. "I'll bet you could hear the ocean if you really tried."

Lee stumbled over a root and Mckenzie steadied him quickly.

"You okay?" he said.

"Yeah. I'm fine. Did you know they hit my nose?"

"Your nose?"

Lee sniffed, then winced. "Yeah. The Japs. They just shot Brenner, right next to me. I felt the impact of the bullet hitting him, I was so close. And then they whacked me, with the butt of their gun. On the nose. Took my gun. I think I could have gotten away, or killed all three of them, had it not been for the fact that they hit my nose. The entire time they were pulling me out into the forest, my nose was bleeding. And I was touching it, and it was bleeding a lot, so I figured it was broken. But it also felt a bit deformed. So I figured my price for living would be a screwed up nose."

"It's looking nice now," John said. "You could win a picture show with that honker."

Lee scratched at the dried blood on his upper lip. "Yeah. Ha ha."

"You look like a clown. You've got a clown nose now," Joe added.

Mckenzie was struck by a sudden wave of guilt. He was just thinking about one fight he had gotten into at school with this one boy who really pissed him off. He punched the boy particularly hard in the nose, and he saw the blood dripping to the tile floor, and he felt vindictive.

Suddenly, he could have vomited. Suddenly, his spirits had lowered, and he was feeling bad, very bad and strange. Did he kill any of those Japs, or had it been John or Joe's shots that killed them? The part of him that simply *didn't know* the answers to those questions was killing him. His last meal rose in his throat, and he forced it down. And he continued to walk.

Ants ate the bottom of his feet. His cells grew bulbs of poison.

"Did I ever really tell you guys about the draft law?" he said.

—

They were very close to the beach, close to where they had been unharmed twenty-four hours ago, when they heard the sounds.

It was gunfire of course. Machine guns, grenades, simple rifles, whatever else. The four men stopped in their tracks.

"Oh, shit," Joe said. His freckled skin grew six shades paler. "Oh, fuck."

"We gotta go. They've started without us."

"Did you think they would wait for us?" Lee said.

Mckenzie clamped his hands over his chest. He was having an unusual bout of heartburn, and his friends' sarcastic bits were killing him.

"What do we do?"

"What do you mean?" Joe said. "We've got to help. There's not much else we can do."

"How long have they been going at it?"

"Doesn't matter," said Lee.

"Where's the enemy coming from?"

Mckenzie groaned.

"They should be coming east again. Like last night."

"We're positioned on the beach. Driving them back."

"Yes, yes. We know. Fuck."

The four men started to jog toward the sounds of fighting.

"Encircle them. Bomb them out. Knock them down," said Lee, slightly out of breath.

They ran faster. They stopped where the dirt forest reached sand. Trees curved down, brushing their heads with leaves. Nobody in their sights were on the beaches, but they could hear the proof that human life was near. Mckenzie raised his gun and checked their surroundings. No Japs lying in wait nearby. He was a child. He knew he was young, but he really *felt* eighteen, right then. How much of what he had learned would help?

"We're on our side," said John.

Joe turned to them and walked backwards a few steps. "I'm going," he said. "I'm gonna find Vicky and Dorman. I'll get you guys when this is done." And brandishing his weapon, Joe sprinted, ducking as he did so, out onto the beaches.

Lee, John, and Mckenzie froze.

"What did he mean by that, that he'll get us when this is done?"

"I'm not staying here," Lee said.

"We can't stay here," said Mckenzie.

"Stop."

Mckenzie looked at John. His voice was tight; his eyes were wary. He was staring, entranced, to the left.

A Japanese soldier was leaning, slouching almost, against a tree. His Army cap covered his eyes and forehead. Instantly, Mckenzie aimed his gun and flew for the trigger.

"Stop," John whispered. "He's dead, anyhow. Don't waste any more ammunition. We're fucking running low at this point."

Slowly, John approached the corpse.

And it all happened very fast.

The corpse was aiming his gun, there were two loud shots, both at the same second and completely indistinguishable from each other, and the Jap fell face down onto the dirt. Lee was shooting repeatedly, and they were all stepping backwards, stumbling, the sudden shock of adrenaline clearing their expressions. And then the high-tension moment was over, so that they could understand what had happened. John St. Dennis collapsed on his back, his head just barely reaching the beach's sand, and Lee and Mckenzie stood over him, watching the front of their friend's Army jacket stain red.

42.

June 16th. Twelve p.m.

Lee was rocking back and forth on his knees, his pants layered in mud, and Mckenzie was thinking, not me, not me, not me, not me—

It was too late for pleasantries. John was going to die. But, I had thought, for just one moment, that I could find some way around that.

God-fearing, I said.

"You're bleeding," said Lee. "It's only a little though, you're okay. It's fine. Go on and get up."

They were kneeling on either side of John, who was laying on the ground. His knee was bent up at an odd angle that Mckenzie thought could be painful, so he pushed it down. The expression on John's face remained the same.

"Wipe it off," John said. "I've got that guy's blood on me, get it off." He was pale, steadily losing color, and he was covered in blood, blood coming from the hole in his chest, staining his letters to home and his little, bulletproof Bible. The Jap's blood mixed with his. The bullet hit the enemy's skull straight on, so that he was completely still in seconds and collapsed on the ground ten feet away. Mckenzie looked at his gun. It had a strange, oily, red, and purple substance on the mouth. He couldn't do it anymore. He'd admit with a straight face that he had given up. He would kill himself and sleep for a while.

He had wanted war to give him something to live for. Now he wanted to die.

John was still breathing even after taking a bullet to his aorta, and he was crying now, feeling at his chest where the liquid was spilling out, and his eyelashes were gluing themselves to his eyelids, his tongue feeling sticky to his palette.

Mckenzie felt an odd sensation on his hands. He looked down to see them repeatedly lifting his canteen, pouring water over the wound. He had a needle of morphine. He was stabbing it into John's thigh. Pressing down onto the wound with anything they had, and the blood was running over his fingers, why was it so warm if death was so, so cold—

"Fucking help, you fucking idiot, you son of a—what the fuck are you doing, you fucking…" muttered Mckenzie to Lee, who was staring at the sun. No angry words were enough. He rocked onto his back, balanced on his bent knees and screwed his eyes up tight to relieve how much he wanted to kill them both and himself. The scraping in his throat told him that he was groaning or crying or something, but the noise was still not helping. He wanted to scream, but if he screamed, the bad guys would be back and they'd make him watch them shoot John in the head this time, and get it right, and spiral off Lee's kneecaps. Cutthroat, peacetime murder was beautiful now. There was nothing left in the world for him, nothing left to see or create; he had seen it all. There was no beautiful rival of strength, no artistic form big enough to combat himself. He'd die as a colorless killer, his last meager desires buried alongside of him, his belongings packed up in a box and sent to the attic. He wanted to be executed for capital murder and be filled up with a substance never meant for the human body. He wanted a last word and he wanted to know it was coming. He wanted to inject himself with it; he wanted to stand before himself in a faceless covering and shoot in unison with the other powerless killers who did not have a choice.

Mckenzie wanted to die and he wanted it quick. He wanted it to be his own death and not in someone else's hands.

He was pressing down on the wound and John was crying, calling Lee's name, Lee who was crowing like a bird. A bird about to be fucking shot, Mckenzie thought, his brain talking clear as day.

"Lee, you—help, will you help, stop crying, you want him to die?"

Four hands were now on John's torso, pressing down.

Oh my god, thought Mckenzie. *He's gonna die.*

And his brain—it snapped. I am not the best writer in the world, and I hope to myself I will never experience the kind of agony we have put these boys through, and I will never be able to explain it adequately. He wanted to live, he wanted to live so he could die with Telly and his school friends and his paintings and his teachers and neighbors, his father, his mom. He wanted to live and he was thinking now very fast, because he could see that John could not, and would never, ever, live again.

John was never too young to die. How could he be, when he was too young to have lived?

"Lee," said Mckenzie suddenly, for he could hear the thundering footsteps. "Lee, we've got to go."

"What?"

"We have to go. They'll get us, Lee, c'mon!" The last word was a sob. "John's dead, Lee, he's dead— "

Lee gave a scream of horrifying tremors that Mckenzie knew he'd never forget, and threw his arms around John's body, completely still. Mckenzie was not looking. He had watched his biggest protector die and now he was truly, truly alone. John's big ears were still intact. He didn't have that excited color to his face. His eyes were open and wet and blue still, still blue in death, if you can imagine. But they were cold and didn't blink back and Mckenzie was wondering if his face hurt, if Harry Houdini *was*, in fact, a mind reader. He was wondering when the Japs would come and stomp John's cracking grape eyes into the ground, and when the planes would hit and bury them all into the dust. In fifty years, there'd be a little white cross over John's remains. He wondered why they ever had to fucking meet.

"John?" he said.

"I'm not leaving, you fucking bastard, go kill yourself, go off now." Lee's eyes were red behind the brown, the dull brown, snot trailing down onto his lips.

"You're gonna die! They're fucking coming, please, Lee! We have to go!" They were crying.

Lee did not move.

Dear loved one.

I have told this story, this urban legend, to friends of a friend. I have written it down a thousand times, in thoughts and conversations, in paint and pencil. I pray that this is the last time I will ever, ever mention this day.

Mckenzie left him.

He left and began walking as fast as his weakened legs could go without the joints splitting at the knee, walking toward the fighting and the raining of metal and blood. Then he ran. He ran, and when he looked back, far behind, he saw the outline of two enemies in the forest standing over a corpse and a kneeling boy. Mckenzie knew it all. Lee was down, and he would be the one to live. In seconds, those three figures were down.

He never talked to John or Lee again.

Dear loved one.

I have told this story, this urban legend, to friends of a friend. I have written it down a thousand times, in thoughts and conversations, in paint and pencil. I am tired. Shamefacedly, I say that I am tired.

Mckenzie was shot in the heart running into his old self in the very heart of the battle. Because I was there, I can say that no heart had ever hurt as such as his did in that moment.

He was laying and dying on the ground.

He was in the hall of a ship vessel. He was screaming for his mother. Man screams for, above all, those who love him.

He was looking up at the sky. It was foggy. Mckenzie noticed that one particular cloud of dust retained a shape that looked like an abstract painting he made before. He had made the painting years ago and forgotten about it mostly. It wasn't his best, but Mckenzie remembered it now.

Dear Loved One.

There was a long empty space of molten bodies forming together to make one tragically alien setting. Death was no uncommon scene. Somewhere over the stretch of land, a blonde-haired soldier was rubbing his dull brown eyes, and coming to consciousness.

43.

June 18th.

Happy Wednesday. He woke to his alarm with a tranquil feeling early that morning. He dressed for work, and for the first time in a while, Telly fixed his tie correctly on the first try.

It was cold for June. Or maybe it was from his early rising. He let his fingertips rest on the chilled window and drank a mug of water. No coffee. He detested coffee.

Breakfast was next, and he ate standing by the kitchen counter, listening to an ad on the radio. His sink was empty for the first time in weeks. He enjoyed it when they played "I'll Be Seeing You." He put the song at the top of his list, and he thought of seeing June, old June, in a cafe, drinking her lovely coffee in a mug. She was always singing in his thoughts. He couldn't help that. When he pictured June, he saw her face tilted back in giddy glee, and her mouth falling open with laughter, mixing up the words in her kerosene-croaking voice.

It was by far the prettiest Wednesday of the year. The flowers were pretty and overgrown over his front steps instead of irritating. The exact wonderful amount of sunlight glued itself to Telly's back as he headed toward town. He was dazed with images of rings and little boys with little pillows in suits. He imagined the new color palette he would get at the store. He would examine it in fuller detail driving to work.

There were two things he saw at once. Number one: the town square was quiet for ten in the morning, and he realized that was because the town hall bell was not ringing ten times. The second thing he saw was Mr. and Mrs. Rye talking to a teenage boy on a bike outside the grocery store, where Telly had first met them. The paper boy wasn't holding a bundle of newspapers. He was holding a yellowed paper out for the couple's eyes.

That's not a paper boy, thought Telly.

I could feel his brain through my fingers, my hand on his head, patting, and I could feel the exact moment when he realized it, and when he started to wonder why it had not crossed his mind before. He did not notice me. But I was crying with him.

I once heard a phrase that has been told in many churches, in classified steeples from the early days, in vacant lots and funeral parlors. Somebody once told me that God cries with you, and although I've grown old and long forgotten the faces of those I've loved, I've never forgotten the words I chose to live by.

—

Telly had gotten close enough to understand what the yellow paper said.

He was back inside his house. He stopped once he shut the front door behind him, and he stood there, staring at the wooden ground for a minute. Then he reached for his telephone.

He sat on the floor and pulled the telephone set in front of him. He dialed the office of the school where he lectured and told them he would not be coming in today because he had some sort of an emergency. Then he called Rico.

"Rico Romano," said his best friend.

"Rico," said Telly.

"Telly, what's going on? You called my work number." The sound of a reclining chair was heard under his voice.

"I'm sorry. Can you put Carrie on?"

"Yeah, yeah. I'm working from home while we unpack."

"I know. Can you put her on?"

"I'll give you the other telephone number and you can call that one."

Rico gave it to him and he hung up. Telly dialed the number. The phone was picked up on the other side very fast.

"Telly, hi," Carrie said.

"Hi." Telly rubbed a hand over his face.

"Telly, what's wrong?"

"Nothing. No. I don't know. The kid's dead."

"What? Hold on, I'm holding boxes and the baby's crying. Hold on."

There was some shuffling and a baby's gibberish. Telly drew a shaky breath.

"Okay, okay. Telly, what's the matter?"

"The kid's dead."

There was some staticky silence.

"Telly, what kid?"

"Mckenzie. He's dead. I saw his parents get the news."

"When?"

"Maybe an hour ago. No, that's not right. Maybe a few minutes ago. I don't know. They got the paper thing, I don't know. I saw them read it and I heard them crying about something."

"A telegram?"

"I don't know."

"Okay. Are you sure?"

"Sure about what?" he said.

There was another silence.

"Telly. Are you sure Mckenzie is dead?"

He nodded, then realized that Carrie could not see the gesture. "Yes. I heard his parents saying stuff. Now what?"

"Okay," she said, "Okay. If you get a funeral invite, then you should go, Telly. It'll be soon, I'm sure."

"Carrie. Now what?"

Silence.

"I don't know. You get a funeral invite, you go. Okay?"

"Okay." And he hung up because he felt that he could no longer endure the sound of her collected and cool voice. She was so wise and he was so not. He tried to imagine how this time in life, for it surely was difficult, would help him in his later years. He thought that no matter how hard your life has been, sometimes you won't be prepared.

He put the telephone back in its proper place. And then he went to his kitchen and looked at the empty sink. Usually he left dishes piled up for a while until he was forced to confront them. But lately he was being tidy. There was no distraction now.

So he was looking down at his sink, one lone China plate in there, a dish his mother forced on him some day that he could not recall, and he was looking, and it was looking back at him, and when he started to cry, it was barely any real tears. It was the guilt inside of him coming, and he didn't know what he was mourning anymore: the loss of Mckenzie, or the loss of his clean hands.

44.

Weeks went by. Mrs. Rye had taken to her bedroom; Mr. Rye was sitting on the couch. He was trying his best to entertain an old school friend. One of Mckenzie's old school friends, that was. He knocked on their door that evening with a basket of canned food Mr. Rye knew the boy's mother had prepared, a letter of condolence, and a request to help with funeral plans.

His name was Stan. He was a year younger than Mckenzie, and they had met through a shared class, which Stan told Mr. Rye lots about. He gave the gift basket to him, then the letter, and told him very straightforwardly his plan to help.

"I could send the invites," said Stan. "Or find a nice church. There's some nice ones in town, if you'd like that, sir, and Mrs. Rye would."

Mr. Rye was finding it slightly difficult to focus on the seventeen-year-old's words. He was busy thinking about what he ate for dinner a few weeks ago. It was good meat, and for dessert, one of those reddish-brown rubbery cakes that tasted like vanilla and cherry. They ate enough for Mckenzie and looked at old photographs and got a bit drunk, but the good kind, the rejoicing kind, like they were celebrating their son's existence instead of mourning his absence. It was Mckenzie's favorite kind of cake on a rare occasion, and since he had been gone, Mr. and Mrs. Rye were eating that cake ten times more than usual.

"I'm friendly with the priest of that one church down the road."

Mr. Rye smiled. "That'd be fine."

"What would be?"

Mr. Rye pushed his glasses up his nose and sighed. He gave up on pretending to have listened. "Stan, how was that class you were telling me about? The one you had with my son."

"Very good, sir. Well, I shouldn't lie, I don't like school much. But it was alright. Not very good," Stan said. Then he looked regretful.

"Was Mckenzie any good at it? Did he have a good grade?"

"Oh, yes. He was really good at math."

"It was a math class?"

"Calculus. I hated it, but now I'm done with it. Mckenzie was good at math. So he had a good letter, I think."

"Stan," said Mr. Rye. He pushed his glasses up again and felt very weary and old. "Stan, it's getting late. Why don't you come back another day, if you'd like?"

"Okay, Mr. Rye. If I can help," Stan said. He got up and slowly backed toward the door. "Thanks, sir. And I'm sorry for your loss." He was genuine.

"Thank you," said Mr. Rye. And Stan left. Mr. Rye was left sitting alone on the couch in his living room with his wife locked in the bedroom and his son dead in a box in some country, somewhere he didn't know about.

That was what he truly found insufferable about the whole ordeal. He knew nothing of Allies and Axes. He knew nothing of God or heaven and hell. How was he supposed to find his son when it was time?

He choked and buried his face into his knees and sobbed weakly. Never had he cursed his nugatory knowledge until now, when he was screaming for someone to make it *fair* and nobody could, not him or his wife, not anyone in town because they weren't there. His boy didn't die from a shot to the heart; it wasn't over quick enough, it wasn't like falling asleep, he didn't just *simply* die. It hurt more than a kid should endure when the worst he ever took was a broken nose, as painful as seeing the boys you grew up with in hard hats, taut-chinned, and bearing what?. Mckenzie took it all in, thinking he had the same chance as everyone else, but the same as everyone else would not be enough. In the end, it didn't matter who he was. All that mattered was chance. And now Mr. Rye was screaming in his head and the really, truly insufferable part was that he could not let the poison out through his mouth, which would never speak a hopeful word again.

"Ed."

Mr. Rye turned around. He didn't bother fixing his ruined face. His wife was standing at the top of the staircase in her pajamas. She had been wearing those pajamas since June 18th. It had been three days since she had moved from her bed.

Mrs. Rye came down the stairs, and the couples' birdlike eyes met, eyes strangely a very similar color, both blinking at tears, and noticing the graying in their hair. They accepted it would have to happen without Mckenzie.

They held each other, touched hands and foreheads, because they could not hold him. Because they did not lose a soldier, or a man. They lost a son.

I watched this scene unfold and I thought of surreal art, and I thought, if I could, I would ask Mckenzie to pretend he was still there.

45.

The surmise of our plot had stretched out thin, and I found myself wanting to see it from the beginning. I wanted to scratch each word out and replace it with new ones. I wanted to drag the lore out from under my tongue and spin what I was told. Desperately, more than anything, I wished I had never seen 1945 unravel.

I asked many a friend if there was anything to that year at all. If the Roman calendar decided to close its shutters after New Year's, I would not complain. Worldwide tensions would have to heighten without me, but I would be silent, crossing the days off until another year arrived, and we would have to brace it again. I thought of the men and women who came before me, took a pencil in their hands, and wrote the course of history down. I thought of them and I took a pencil and began my letter. I addressed no one but those who I misguided.

I'd bet that Mckenzie did not go to heaven or hell, if you believe in such. His days were so longingly short, so short that only until the end did he wish for an extension. There was no chance to hurt his fate, or increase his landings in heaven. I gave him no chance.

And as I started to write it all down for you, I thought about how if I ever touched you, you would never know. I rediscovered my alliance with you, and your friends and your lovers. I vowed never to watch again. I vowed to overturn that vile checkerboard, to crush each and every emblem of royalty, to cross into the other world with your hand in mine. I swore on this and yet I knew it was futile. I had been envisioning a clean future for them all, until I saw the shapes behind the fog were people. There was no chance for *me*. I could not give what they all desired so deeply in their bodies. There was nothing left to give, and after watching the pawns being buried over and over, I went to the torched field, the field of crosses, and met with your ghosts.

46.

He found the invite in his mailbox. His presence was requested at the church in town, ten a.m., June 22nd. It had been six days since Mckenzie's recorded death, and it was the second invitation he had received from the Ryes. The very day of the funeral, unknown to anyone in town, General Ushijima and General Cho killed themselves in ritual unity, and the battle of Okinawa was over.

—

Telly got to the church at exactly ten and forgot to be proud of himself. He parked in the lot and noted the number of vehicles. Mckenzie was liked, Telly knew this, but he made it out as though he wasn't. He saw a group of high school boys, maybe seniors who had just graduated, huddled together outside the church, shoulders shaking. Telly thought for a split second that they were laughing.

It was a beautiful Catholic church, and he supposed that Mckenzie had known it in his days. That was the painful part, maybe. He didn't know. But it appeased his eyes, that was all, and his first view of it was through the large circular entryway. He was elbowed aside; he was frozen, stuck, staring at the magnificent architecture, the glorious glass and angles of it all, his bored, uncaring asshole demeanor caving in as he pressed one hand experimentally hard against a window, so when he turned away, his fingers were yellow under the skin. Strangely enough, Telly was taking in this big piece of artwork as the most influential sight he could have been met with. He was also beginning to feel that he was more selfish than he had thought. Death sometimes causes this.

He chose a pew in the back where it was most open; the person closest to him was a woman in the row across from him. He wondered how she knew Mckenzie. He could *see* Mckenzie, the curves of his face and nature of his words in the lines on the ceiling. Lines. It was a mural, but he had reduced it to lines.

"Heaven is crying tears today," said a priest, the noise echoing off the high walls, and Telly realized it had started, and that he was spacing out, that he could see a group of boys hiding their faces in the second row, and the back of Mr. and Mrs. Rye's heads in the first.

And the priest was talking, waving his hands sadly at the front of the room, and Telly smelled a strange metallic scent, like blood, and he was thinking, *Sick, sick, sick. I feel sick.*

He spotted the coffin through a gap between the guests. Was it full? Had that coffin ever been used before? Was it even closed? Telly was thinking all these things and then he was thinking, *Sick, sick, sick. This is sick.* He was thinking that, yes, they could all go and talk about Mckenzie's life, but no one could talk about his death, because nobody understood. Nobody cared.

His father was talking.

His friend, his best friend, was talking.

Someone else now.

And Telly was leaving, walking numbly out the church door as the ceremony ended, being followed by the others who were not close with Mckenzie's parents, not close enough to offer deep sincerity. When Telly turned around, watching the gathering of guests leaving the funeral, he noticed that there weren't, in fact, a lot of guests. He compared the number of mourners to the number of cars in the parking lot. Then he realized. The church was right next to some sort of store, and at the moment, Telly saw that it was a very popular venue. June called just as he walked in the door of his house. Somehow he found an excuse to hang up.

The month went like this until its end.

July.

5

July began like this:

He would wake at the exact time his alarm went off, and the days became hotter. Long gone were the tranquil, lusty fixtures of the flowers swinging over his front step; they drooped into the grass, their muzzles saturated with sweet sweat and morning dew that dried up in seconds. The Rye home was on Telly's route to work. He found himself taking the longer way after seeing the melted, charred candles in their yards. And although it was hot, for the first four days of July, it rained.

On July Fourth, Harry Truman gave some sort of address and Telly didn't listen to it. Instead, he listened to the neighbors down the street light fireworks for the children who were surely running barefoot in overalls. The next morning, he opened the windows and tasted nothing but the burnt aftermath and the empty facade of an American residence. He recovered his good sense midday. He returned June's calls with the barest regards.

The rain was so ponderous that it was a miracle any oxygen was able to penetrate it at all, and the only kind was a thick layer of perspiration, or the aftertaste of that rain. In the future, Telly would forget the end of June and beginning days of July, but he would never forget that rain. Each morning he felt it return with greater vindication, and by night it was secreting and boring its way into his lungs. He breathed in a craving for normalcy and humid, messy atmosphere.

Telly received his final letter from the Ryes at the beginning of the month. It was not an invitation this time, and he recognized the packaging of such a letter before recognizing the writer's handwriting, for he had gotten a similar letter before. It was addressed differently, however.

Telly, it said.

He ignored the stamp of approval on the worn paper and studied the letter before reading. It was dated early June. Telly thought that the delivery time was ironic. There was also a photograph in the envelope. Telly pulled it out. In it was a group of men, maybe fourteen of them, all mostly young and wearing Army greens in front of some building. They weren't smiling, but they looked proud. Mckenzie was on the far right. The photo was captioned from left to right: Private Halsted, Private Dorman, Private White, Private Marshall. And so on. Telly studied Mckenzie's face, until he realized he was trying to see if the kid had changed. He put the photograph aside and began to read the letter.

Telly,

I signed your name this time. I've decided that the government would not want much to do with you anyhow, so it doesn't matter. I don't know when you will get this, but I do know that America is a day or so behind us, so as I am writing this, it is the past day for you. Get it?

There are a lot of men out here. Most of them have been here for a while, but we've only been in Okinawa for maybe two weeks. I easily lose track of time, and for a while, I forgot I had a watch and attempted to teach myself how to tell time through the sun, like in ancient cultures. But the sun has not been cooperative. It's just not coming out. I've been told by men who've been here since April that May was much better than they expected. And then we showed up and it all got ruined. So I can't see the sun very well at all and it's muddy. You could argue that the mud keeps you warm, but when the temperature rises, it gets really hot and uncomfortable. And at night it is cold.

My friend Lee, who I think I told you about, is doing well. He's actually doing better than the rest of us, and I think it's because he is smarter than the rest of us. He's really a smart kid, and he's a year older than I, and I don't think he's ever made a mistake once in his life, he is so rock solid. I admire that about him. My friend John is not doing well, I don't think. Half the time he's got this weird look on his face and doesn't look like himself. John's older than me by a year also, but he's acting young. He's all out of sorts and I can't find a way to help him out much when I know some men are much worse.

I am currently wishing that everything at home is going nicely. When you write back, tell me some more stories like you did in your last letter, and tell me if you have finished any paintings yet. I bet you haven't. You get no work done most of the time, I don't know how you can count as an adult. But I told John and Lee and some other guys about you and told them that you think if you ever got married, your wife would kill you. They thought that was really funny. I guess other people think you're funny, but maybe if they were there when you said it, they'd know you're a horrible joker.

From,
          Mckenzie.

That time, he signed his name.

—

Later that night, Telly called June. He subconsciously had been lessening their time spent together, until he had not seen her in two weeks. He couldn't bring himself to feel bad about this. He just didn't feel very much for himself at the moment, so he couldn't feel something for her.

He heard through the phone that she was upset. He didn't blame her. Still, Telly found himself giving an oily excuse to hang up, and when he was left alone with the silence of his own house, he closed his eyes to rekindle that feeling he had when he was looking at June that other night. How pretty she looked among his artwork and his kitchen and his pillows and his books. She was making everything else look nicer, and when she was gone, he embraced the loss and loved the heartfelt pain. But now Telly was thinking that America was about a day behind Japan, and that when he had been watching June sleep in his bed with a sin-sickly, lover's grin on his face, Mckenzie could have been dying at the same moment.

He cursed himself to be a lone widower. Sometimes death doesn't bring out a stronger love between two. Sometimes it brings out the honesty.

48.

"*I don't* understand," said June. "What's going on?"

They were standing in the bright lamp light of June's kitchen, in her little flat a few towns over. She had just gotten home from a shift and was still wearing her waitress apron. Telly was expecting this. He was hoping that the sight of the uniform would inspire any response of emotion in him, but still he was feeling nothing. June's confusion only caused a slight infliction of annoyance in Telly that he quickly brushed away.

"I can't be in love if I don't know what love is," Telly said.

June frowned. "Well, firstly, I don't know *what* you're talking about. And secondly, that's not true."

"It's not?"

"No, it's not," she said, "You're supposed to learn what love is with someone you love."

"Are we in love?" he asked quietly.

"I don't know."

"See? You don't know. How can we ever be in love if we don't know now?"

"Telly," she scoffed. "Why the hell do you wanna know everything? You're not going to. Now, what's going on?"

Telly felt one last vapid twist of affection before every trace of it was gone, and he was left with just himself to confront.

"June," he said. He pushed his hands into his pockets. "June, we've got to break up."

Her reaction was instantaneous, and in that moment, Telly knew she had been expecting this, had been thinking this over, and he knew that deep down, she would feel the same way someday if they stayed together.

Had she ever been as bright as he remembered? Had *he*?

"So that's what this has all been about?" she said, but she didn't sound angry. "Give me your reasons and I'll let you go on."

"June, it's like wearing a shirt that's too small," he said carefully.

"So you've grown too big for me? That's it? You've gotten sick of me, have you?" she said, and *now* she was angry. She clenched her teeth, her brown eyes lightening in the hazy kitchen atmosphere, her long, knobby legs standing painfully straight.

He was stuck with no words, wondering how she could be so unapologetically, beautifully human, wondering why he was so flawed, flawed enough to see what he wanted in everything, instead of seeing past the nitpicky, handpicked devices that tortured him day and night.

"That's not it."

"No?"

"June, how can I be with someone when I can hardly be with myself?"

"You're saying you don't like yourself? That's your reason?"

"No!" he said loudly. "I can't be with anyone! I can't do anything. I met you and I thought that I could. I thought I would be a famous artist and make loads of cash, and now I'm owning up to the fact that I'm fucking average and my love is fucking average! And we don't love each other—"

"Love? When were we thinking about love?"

"See, that's just it, June! We weren't talking about love, but I'm so low all the time that I think every normal emotion is a side effect of being in love, and I know I like you a lot, but I can't stay with someone I'll end up loving, because I can't love anyone right now. I won't be able to for a while, June." He begged her to understand.

"Telly, not everything has a very philosophical answer," June snapped. "You're not in anyone's life. Have you considered you're low from loneliness?"

"I had everyone I needed," Telly said.

"Had? You think you don't need any human connections *now*? When will you stop leaving people?"

"I leave people?" His intensive anger was tipping over into calamity, and his throat was beginning to hurt. "I leave people? June, everyone's left *me!*"

"You're leaving me. You complain of being left? Then why do you leave *everyone?*"

"I'm *not!*"

"Telly, have you ever thought that no one is leaving you? You see someone trying to make something out of themselves and you think that means they're leaving you behind, and you leave. That's what you do," she said.

She was right, too. She was always right. That was something he hadn't made up.

Still, he was shaking his head but agreeing with her words, and then he was walking out her front door. It was that July kind of chilly outside and he enjoyed it for a split second. He turned back around to look at June standing in the frame of her door, leaning against the archway. Telly knew that they had both calmed down at this point, that they were both feeling the same breeze, and in years to come, they would both understand the whole of each other.

"When will we stop leaving each other?" said June.

"This is the last time. Thanks for everything, June." And he meant it. He let her close the door behind him without looking back. He had a habit of looking back at her.

He drove home and thought about all he had not told June. He didn't turn off the radio; he just switched the volume down. It was playing a nice musical beat. And he thought about how he hadn't told her about Mckenzie, how she knew little to nothing about him, because Telly thought that *he* knew nothing about him. They said teenage boys wanted nothing besides heroics, but they were wrong.

And Telly was thinking about Mckenzie's letter, and how in all of his letters he was so wise. He was positive there was a place in his chest where his organs had been punctured and squished; he felt it whenever he thought of Mckenzie. Because thinking of Mckenzie meant thinking of the world's greatest injustices. Mckenzie, who never died a sweet sleep, who was hurt until every man who looked on was just the doctor, and he the patient. Still Telly was thinking that there was nothing to know, that all there was to be discovered was that Mckenzie died. Still was he thinking of that letter and the photograph that came with it.

Something was clicking oddly in his head.

John's a new friend of mine, and Lee. They've got the same funny accent as you.

That first letter from May.

From left to right.

That photograph.

Private St. Dennis, Private Rye, Private Collins.

Who were they?

Telly frowned. An accent?

49.

He did understand now.

That weekend, Telly and his letter and his labeled photograph drove to Boston and parked at the first newspaper office he found. He demanded politely to speak to a team editor. He waited patiently until the editor arrived. Then he showed him the letter and the photograph. He told the editor the plan. And the editor agreed. Telly watched him converse briefly with a nearby journalist, and Telly left the office empty-handed.

Telly made sure to look at the Boston newspapers the next week. He was thinking of funny Massachusetts accents, accents Telly shared with two nineteen-year-olds from the same city. And on the third page of the paper, he saw it. A short tabloid, complete with a photograph of Mckenzie's gift. And finally, the story ended with a call for the families of Private St. Dennis, and Private Collins, or the very men themselves, to step forward and explain what happened the day of June 17th, 1945.

A funny accent.

A *Boston* accent.

—

It was simple once Telly understood what to do. Mckenzie had told him that Lee Collins and John St. Dennis had accents similar to his own. Telly did not understand such a notion, and for a while, he stood in front of the mirror and said "car," repeatedly.

So he *did* have an accent.

And John and Lee had the same one as him.

And Telly was *from* Boston. So, hopefully, Lee and John were also from Boston. And, yes, he knew it was a huge city and there was a possibility that they didn't even live there anymore—there was the possibility that they had moved off the grid, or their families were dead, or they were still at war. There were many limitations. But Telly had to try. He wanted to *understand*.

There it was again. His apparent *fatal* flaw: the desire to understand all. Why did he have such a wanting? After all these months, he was beginning to see. He felt as though an isolated acre of his mind had found sunlight, and finally there was something growing in the malnourished organ, something to breathe life into the lifeless form. If there was a meaning to life, he had not found it. But he was slowly realizing something about himself. When he saw the future through a kaleidoscope, he saw nothing. He saw the present. He saw Christmas with Carrie and Rico, painting with Mckenzie, teaching obscure visions of art, teaching and dancing and painting, singing along to the words. To some, this is nothing. This used to be true for Telly. But now, this was his everything. It was his past and future. He held everything inside of him.

"This is it, isn't it?" said Telly. There was nobody else in the room. I realized with shock that he was talking to me.

In July he waited for a response. He studied the icy blue sky and its swift afternoon storms. He felt the crisp presence of summer and longed for fall.

By August 1st, enough word had gotten into the locals. The Boston newspaper office telephoned Telly with the good news: The St. Dennis family had seen the paper and agreed to a meeting. The bad news was that John St. Dennis had been dead since June.

August.

6

They met at a small, unpopular cafe at the halfway mark, Telly and the two parents without the son. It was a Sunday at ten in the morning. When asked, the couple said they could meet on a Sunday. They didn't go to church anymore.

Telly arrived at the cafe early, but Mrs. St. Dennis was already seated. The cafe was run by young women with dried, pale faces, and drawn-out eyes. They cleaned the tables with bleak rags and slow, loose movements.

He was brought to the correct table by a hostess who walked off before Telly could thank her. Mrs. St. Dennis was the only person at the table, and Telly sat across from her, holding his new copy of the photograph in his clenched, sweaty palm.

"My husband's a bit late," she said at seeing Telly's curiosity. She was a long-necked, straight-backed, nearing-middle-aged woman with loosely-curled brown hair and small, pointy eyes. She was the kind of woman to wipe her eyes without shame. "He's been working more often now."

"That's quite alright, ma'am," said Telly. He cleared his throat. "Thanks for meeting me."

"Go on and call me Mariam," she said. With an unnoticeable click of her eyes, she was looking at something behind Telly's back. She pointed, a gesture somehow smooth. "That's him," she said, "My husband's here. His name's Jack."

Telly turned around. Mr. St. Dennis was at the hostess stand and being directed to the table. He was tall and strong, his beard sculpted into a slight point at the end of his wide jaw, his teeth of average size for such a face, his hair pale brown. He swept his sea hat on his head with the air of a hyper, casual fellow, and I instantly recognized him as the fisherman who once cursed the Japs, who once cursed the bastards, and never went to fish again.

I know you, I said.

The next week, the fisherman returned home from his voyage. The winter would be too cold. He brought his suitcase to the front door of his house and hugged his wife and kid. He cried. And he never went out to sea again.

I remember, I said.

Telly didn't know it, but in the flesh, Jack St. Dennis was the spitting image of his son.

"Hi," he said first to Telly, and shook his hand; firm, but fast. Then he greeted his wife, patted her shoulder, and sat beside her. He faced Telly.

"We're going into this pretty blindly," Jack said. "We just got a call from a friend; they told us about the paper. And *they* gave us your information."

"Telly," Telly said quickly. "That's what I go by."

"Alright," said Mariam.

"I want to say first that I am very, very sorry about your son," Telly said. The photograph creased in his hand, and he cringed at the awkward noise.

"Thank you," Mariam said.

"I am, too," Jack said and sniffed, frowning at the ceiling. "You like coffee?" Then he ordered three coffees for the table.

"So. A photograph?" Mariam appeared to be x-raying Telly. He briefly thought that this could be the effect of losing a child.

"Yes. Er—yes. Here." He held out the photograph and attempted to decrease the wrinkles.

It was the picture of the fourteen soldiers that Mckenzie had sent him in a letter. From left to right: Private St. Dennis, Private Rye, Private Collins.

"That's John right there," said Jack, and he jabbed at his son. "We got this, too. He sent it to us in one of his first letters."

"All of his words were blacked out. He's a blabber."

"He's telling all of America's secrets," said Jack. "Can you imagine that? John knowing stuff like that?"

Mariam grinned.

"I got this picture in a letter," said Telly. "From Mckenzie. He's right here."

And there was Mckenzie, cramped between the other men. John St. Dennis had one hand extended, just barely touching Lee Collins' shoulder, and the other hand mussing up Mckenzie's hair. They were all trying not to smile, Mckenzie especially, their faces bright and freshly shaven in the spotted black and white. Lee had his head tilted back, chin high in the air, maybe a bit sure, maybe a bit clever. Telly saw that Lee Collins maybe had a bit of what he himself desired: that *understanding*.

"Your brother?" asked Mariam.

"No. I was his tutor."

"Tutor in what?"

"Art, actually. He was a great painter. Much better than me," said Telly, and instantly was ashamed at admitting his worst fear aloud.

"John talked about him," Jack said and leaned back in his seat. "He wrote about Mckenzie and Lee. Those two grew up together since— thank you." Both he and Mariam nodded and thanked the waitress, then instantly slurped their steaming cups.

"He's dead, isn't he?" Mariam said. It was not a question.

Telly nodded and cleared his throat again. "Yes. On June 17th."

"That's when John died. He died June 17th." Jack's words were very fast, Telly noticed. He kept his words short.

"Yeah. I wanted to maybe understand what had happened. I was just reading Mckenzie's letters. He mentioned your son a lot. And Lee Collins."

"You're from that town?" Mariam said. "That one without the draft? John said something about a friend from there."

Telly suddenly had a strong sense that most women were a lot like Carrie. Mariam didn't question him on particulars of town living.

She did not ask him what he read in the papers every day, or if he listened to the radio. She just moved on.

"We don't understand much of what happened," she said, "We weren't there to see any of it. But we really can't help. John's not here to explain any of it, either."

Telly nodded.

Then Mariam sniffed, and although the photograph did them no justice, her eyes perfectly matched her son's. "But I know someone who can help." She gave him a final address and a name on a napkin. Telly kept that napkin for a long time. Years and years after, the napkin deteriorated into nothing, in the attic of an older man.

51.

"Hi," *Telly said* into the phone, pressing it against his ear with his shoulder as though his hands were full. He sat cross legged on the hardwood floor of his tiny house exactly as he had two months ago. By now the air had increased in its heat, so that the walls were no longer like chilled icing at the touch. He wore no socks and nice clothes. He had started going back to work a while before.

It was a change from the last time. Carrie had called him. Easily, he was picturing her blonde, light-weighted hair, her pale, gleaming pallor. He wished she had never been touched by war in such a strange way. He wondered how many lifetimes she would go through where everything repeated.

"Hi," said Carrie. "I wanted to hear how you were doing."

"You know, I'm doing good," he said.

"Yeah?"

"Carrie," he said. "I am."

"Okay. I believe you."

"Carrie, I talked to some people recently."

"Some people?" she said, and Telly could sense her curiosity behind the cautiousness. He felt a rush of affection toward her.

"I wanted to figure some things out. You know, understand what happened to Mckenzie."

There was a short silence. "Yes, go on."

"I found some people who could help me. And they found someone else."

"Telly." She smiled over the receiver. "That's good. I'm glad."

"Anyway, I wanted to say that I'm happy you called. I wanted to tell you and Rico how wonderful you've been."

"Don't give me that."

"No, no. I mean it. You've been better than a person could ask for. And you know something else?" Now Telly began to smile, emotions blurring his eyes, which he was no longer ashamed of. "I'm really glad I met that kid Mckenzie. I really am."

"Me too, Tel."

"I think he taught me a lot. Even if he wasn't here to see me actually comprehend it."

"Wasn't it supposed to be the other way around?" said Carrie, and she was laughing.

Telly shook his head. "I didn't teach him much that was helpful."

"Oh, you did. Trust me, you did."

"I don't know. Maybe." He smiled again, his cheek wet against the phone. "Maybe we'll meet again sometime and he'll tell me if I ever taught him something after all."

"That's sweet."

"What?"

"Saying that. Saying that you'll see him again," Carrie said.

"I read that somewhere, actually," he said. "I read it in this book. This book on spirits and legends, that sort of thing. And the author said that the book was written down a million times until they finally got it right."

52.

Somewhere along the line, there was a story. There was a fisherman who loved his son more than the sea. There was a girl and her brother making joy out of the deprivation. Somewhere along the line, there was a whistling man with a list of names, and the memories of the names before.

Once upon a time, there was a story.

There was a difficult, talented student.

There was an open and closed teacher.

There were two boys from Boston who wrote their own way.

I say to you now. There is no such thing as endings; there is no such thing as death. We live on in the souls of the people around us, and when there are none left who remember us, we live in the grass and the trees. We are never truly gone when we have so many ties to this world. We are linked to every person in ways unimaginable. There has been no coincidence. We are never forgotten, even if there is little to remember.

Somewhere along the line, a fisherman's son was drafted. He cursed the world and never returned to the ocean again.

Somewhere along the line, a young girl's brother had his birthday called out. He never told them that he had given himself up long before.

Somewhere along the line, a man was reading the names of his latest recruits. He smoked a cigar out the window of his office, so as not to bother anyone.

Once upon a time, there was a teacher and his student. They spent hours arguing nonsense and debating the role of art, until one of them had to go.

This time, I am giving you reassurance. Whatever you touch in your life, whether it is a hat empty of change, a paintbrush, a gun, a fishing line, a car magazine, it will never leave you. Your story is everlasting and ever changing. It is being written into eternity.

My dear loved one. I once saw a rope with a collection of knots. On further inspection, I saw these knots had ties to other ropes, until I saw a thousand ropes, all around me. It is the moments we throw these ropes out into the open sea to save ourselves, that we must remember, stories have no true ending. They just go on.

53.

It was around 3,000 miles away. California was all fractured nitrogen lawns, bloody Fridays, and prefabricated housing, as well as the sapid smell of bursting grapes and yellow pages, in 1945. August sent a crushing heat over the populous cities, until the days were closing into September and the northeast was awaiting fall. They'd have to wait until the following spring to go home.

I have heard that many of them were children. They and their parents roofed under the lifeless barbed caging along with the guards and the others without a penny to their names, and felt at their lonely, stringing belongings. They felt bleak and colorless among the growing Hollywood headlines. Perhaps one hundred years earlier, someone's grandfather had been living a similar way.

The camps were lacking, besides being without due process and identity. At the end of August, Telly was looking at these photographs of them. Someone had taken these pictures and forced themselves to leave the establishment as a lesser American. But he looked at the pictures and read the stories and quotes that went along with them. He was captured by the little girls and boys playing hopscotch without the chalk, in black and white printing, in a black and white world. Instantly, Telly decided that was his very problem; there was no color, and while the entire world was booming with shouldered, rugged prosperity, another life form was being buried underground. He figured that life on canvas was another vision altogether. He figured he could give certain things an oil base and color, and that he would rather paint life than ignore its potential.

Telly knew he no longer had business where he was. He was too busy concentrating on outsider culture to pretend that he belonged. How could he have potential at all if everything there to describe was just beyond his reach? Every conversation he had was about theory past the border of town, and just now he was beginning to realize that he was not being held back at all. He could live his own life if he chose to and he could live without fear in another place, could take his convictions and admissions and grow them elsewhere. Lately, Telly had been talking to himself. This, I saw, was a new development and not one that would falter his decisions. He calculated each reasoning behind his future choices. He asked every part of his being what to do. For once, Telly was beginning to understand that an understanding was without what?. He could quit his responsibility of extraordinary and leave his desire to know and hold everything over the world. He could just exist.

This in itself was a new development, and as Telly began to ponder, really, truly ponder, he searched himself for the ideal future he once invented, and found that he really never had one. Telly went into life with a loose touch, imagined he knew exactly how his life would play out, and now he saw that he never had a concrete plan, never had an exact life schedule. All he knew at a young age was what he loved. And now, Telly knew he could not do what he loved if he remained in town.

For a while, Telly wondered where he would go if he really did leave town. He was facing the fact that he had nobody left, his friends were all gone, and his inspiration had slowly expired. There was no jealousy to put toward a better artist; there was no better artist. I thought that for the first time, Telly was sewing himself into a complete whole. Or maybe he just missed his friends. But Telly pictured Mckenzie's talent leaking into the water with himself standing over as victor, pumping his fists, until seeing that he had lost all that was physical in the journey, that he was merely the illustrator besides the paperback writer, and he had become the kind of person who accepted my fanatics and believed in the rules of humanity.

The rules of humanity; that was the first time I was ever presented with such a theory. It was almost funny to me that the rules set in stone only included *one* rule.

Certain things should not have to happen.

Certain things *should not* have to happen.

And yet, without the continuous, ever moving way of the universe, the connections would have broken between us long ago, and there would be no natural proceedings of time and events. The human goal is not to understand this. It is to accept this.

So, it is true. Certain things happen. But it is not the "*why*" that should keep us up at night. It is the forethought about what to do now that it has happened. It is your reactions that hold up the rope and all of its knots, and as Telly thought this over, my hand on his shoulder, he thought of California.

He thought of California and its fractured nitrogen lawns, bloody Fridays, and prefabricated housing, the sapid smell of the bursting grapes, the yellow pages. How foreign a place like that was to him. And he desired now, instead of an understanding, a liberation. A renewal of color. He wanted to show the unnecessariness of war. He wanted to stop pretending that nothing was happening, that by not participating, he was somehow fixing the world. And if that brought him to California, so be it. He would involve himself so fully, it would be like Mckenzie had never, ever been so alone.

March he was painting a blank canvas. He was eating cake at a party.

April he was playing a game of chess. The queen and king were knocked off the board.

May the Soviets closed the gap. He read letter after letter.

June he fell in love. He waved goodbye to his only friends left.

July he considered his remains. He let the door shut behind him.

August the mourning parents met at a cafe. They gave one final gift. And in that second, looking at the eyes of a woman and her son, he felt closer to me than ever.

Telly wanted a fresh start. Maybe he would move somewhere new.

But first, there was something he had to do. It involved tying the final knot and realizing the rope wouldn't have stayed together without one.

dear loved one,

I have told this story, this urban legend, to friends of a friend. I have written it down a thousand times, in thoughts and conversations, in paint and pencil. I have brought a flashlight to my mouth and spoken in the dark, and the words were never right. It is but a simple story. And so, I will end it by saying that September had never been so tired until 1945.

I must tell you that on September 2nd, on a cold night made for crying, I saw Telly leave his front steps. He got into his car. There was a scrap paper with an address set on his wheel. His loved ones watched him above as he drove. He listened to "I'll Be Seeing You" on the radio and, finding that he knew the words, sang out loud. And he did not pause to question himself until he had passed the highway sign. It welcomed him to Boston.

I should tell you that Telly followed the directions exactly, and as he drove and made his U-turns, he thought of the final address, the last day, the calculated, loving celebration that he had long awaited. He would have to wait just a little longer for it.

It was a small apartment condo in South Boston, a brick building surrounded by its brick brothers and sisters. The windows were quiet and full of warm yellow light in the purple sky that blackened with every minute. What could he do but knock on the door?

So Telly knocked on the door. He did not expect it to open.

A woman, a young girl, for better words, stood behind the door. She was an intellectual with blonde hair and dull, noiseless brown eyes. She had once gone for walks down the streets of Boston with her blonde brother, and had been unable to ignore poverty. She had stolen looks at secret car magazines hidden away in drawers. She had been a lover of birthdays, long ago.

"Who are you?" she asked defensively. "What do you want? I haven't got anything for you."

But Telly had expected such a hello. He nodded politely, as much as he could, being a stranger on her doorstep late at night. And he reached into his jacket pocket and pulled out a photograph that a grieving mother had given him in the weeks before. A labeled picture of three boys, one laughing, one proud, one pulling at the others. He watched her face change in recognition. She knew. She *understood*.

"I will get him," the girl said. She even smiled. "You stay here. Right here."

Telly waited shortly, less than a minute. He was suddenly nervous that she would never return. But she did. And she brought forth a young man into the dim lighting of the streetlamps. He was blonde, brown-eyed, and almost, almost looking bored, with black framed glasses high on his nose. His right leg was tightly bandaged below the knee. He limped now. And he was so beautiful. Truth *can be beautiful*. It only lies in the in-between place. The place of death in life, and life in death, where you can see the words, and your loved ones write letters.

"What's this?" said Lee Collins.

Wordlessly, Telly held up the photograph for him to see.

And easily, Lee remembered. He saw it all before his eyes, every moment of his life, everything he had faced and everyone he loved, everything he had been told, he remembered. He remembered Mckenzie's final tale, his last story told. For they had met before, in another life, in mud and foreign bedsheets, in blood and sand and strange land. There are never any words to describe the final knot being tied, but I have tried my best.

They shook hands on the streets of South Boston, in the cold, crying night. I heard the tears from the other side of the world, from Japan and Germany and England. And on this particular night in 1945, if you looked up, you would have seen September finally closing its eyes and falling asleep. It truly was a sight to see. I wish you had been there.

Love,